WINTER BRINGERS

Also by Gill Arbuthnott

Chaos Clock

Chaos Quest

Dark Spell

For older readers

Beneath

For more information about Gill visit her website at
gillarbuthnott.wordpress.com

WINTER BRINGERS

GILL ARBUTHNOTT

Kelpies is an imprint of Floris Books
First published in 2005 by Floris Books
This second edition 2014

This publisher acknowledges subsidy from Creative Scotland towards the publication of this volume

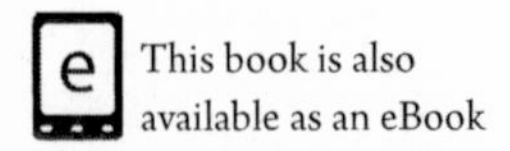

British Library CIP data available
ISBN 978-178250-098-8
Printed in Poland

For James, Calla and les girls
– you know why

PROLOGUE

My name is Agnes Blair. I am sixteen years old and I am afraid. They came for Beatrix and Janet last night and if they do not confess, they will be put to the question. No one stays silent under questioning. They will give me up.

We meant no harm to anyone. We DID no harm to anyone. We did what we did, meaning to help. We wanted to help all the village. If the Minister would just listen to the truth he would see, but he and the others will only listen to what they expect to hear. They will be deaf to the truth.

I am going to write down the truth and hide the papers if they come for me. When they come for me. That way, someone will find out the truth in a week, or a year, or a hundred years.

After they have killed us.

1. Luath

Josh dipped a toe in the water. It was warmer than he had expected. He backed up a couple of steps and took a running jump into the pool, tucking his knees up under his chin so that he hit the water like a cannonball.

The blue underwater silence engulfed and held him for a few seconds, then his head broke the surface and he shook wet hair out of his eyes.

"It's good," he called "Are you coming in?"

"Not like that." His mother took off her white towelling robe and climbed down the ladder into the water. "I hate this bit," she said, slowing down as the water rose up her swimsuit. "It's fine once you're in, but getting there ..." She pushed off and swam across the little pool to Josh.

"That's better."

They stood side by side in the chest-high water, looking out at the field just beyond the path outside, their heads level with the ground.

Cold rain was sheeting in, more horizontal than vertical, hitting the glass in the big windows and streaming down them.

"I'm glad I'm in here and not out there," said Josh.

"Mmnnn ..."

"It's not going to be like this all week, is it?"

She sighed. "I hope not. I don't want you under my feet all the time. The idea was that you and Charlie would be out most of the time enjoying the summer weather together while I worked. I've got to meet that deadline somehow."

That had been the idea, until Josh's best friend Charlie had come off his skateboard and broken his ankle the day before he was supposed to come on this holiday with them. It had sounded much more fun then, but now Josh was wondering what he was going to do for a week stuck in the middle of nowhere.

They watched the rain again in silence for a moment before Josh let himself slide under the water and began to swim.

* * *

They'd arrived at the cottage, part of a small holiday complex, the night before, also in driving rain. They were staying for a week, while his mother, Anna, tried to complete the first draft of a book she was writing on Chartres Cathedral. Most of their luggage seemed to consist of heavy books and files of dog-eared papers which were to emerge by the end of the month, miraculously transformed into neat, coherent print.

They'd come here in particular for two reasons: nostalgia on his mother's part – she had spent her student years at St Andrew's University, just a few miles from the village of Pitmillie where they were staying – and the area's record for weather; much better than

elsewhere in Britain over the run of cold and dreary summers that had been the pattern over past ten years or so, (something that scientists bafflingly attributed to global warming). In the last twenty four hours at least, it had failed to live up to its reputation.

At least there was plenty to do at East Neuk cottages even if it did rain.

After half an hour or so she got out of the pool, leaving him floating on his back, staring up at the ribbed wooden ceiling. After a bit he surface dived and swam a few lengths under water. Even the pool would be more fun with someone else around. He got out and put on the towelling robe to dash back to the cottage through the rain, though why he was bothered about getting wet when he'd just climbed out of a swimming pool was a mystery even to him. When he opened the door however, the rain had gone off and a watery looking sun was trying to force its way through the thinning clouds.

He found Anna hard at work on a pile of papers, her hair sticking in all directions in damp blonde spikes.

"When's lunch?" he asked as he went to get dressed.

She glanced at her watch. "In about an hour. Why don't you go for a walk while the sun's nearly out."

He opened his mouth to say he didn't think he'd bother, but before he could, she went on. "You could walk into the village. There are a couple of things we could do with from the shop." She produced a list she'd already written and gave it to him. He looked at her with narrowed eyes.

"You hate black coffee, so it's as much for your sake as mine. Go on, it won't take you long," she said firmly. "You never know, you might even find you enjoy walking."

"Yeah, right," he said with a scowl, but he didn't really mind: sometimes it was a nice change to have something you had to do.

***

If he could have gone straight over the fields it would only have taken him five minutes, but the way the drive and the roads went he had to walk three sides of a square, so it took fifteen.

At least it wasn't raining. In fact, the sun had gained enough strength for him to take his jacket off and tie it round his waist by the time he'd gone halfway.

It was amazingly noisy. He had expected the countryside to be quiet, but this bit certainly wasn't. Birds were making a racket, cows were mooing, and a tractor taking a clattering path up the road past him was almost deafening him. There was a dog barking close by as well.

That was the sound he concentrated on. He didn't like dogs. Never trusted them, even the little-old-lady dogs that looked like mop heads and seemed to eat nothing but chocolate drops. He reckoned that, secretly, they all had a taste for human flesh, and they'd bite if they had the chance.

He didn't know why he didn't like dogs. (He wouldn't have used the word scared, since he liked to think he'd made a choice about it.) He'd never actually been bitten by one, though his grandad had had a Collie cross that sublimated its sheepdog urges by herding him round the garden with yips and growls, snapping at his heels.

As he walked on, reaching the first houses in the village, he realized that the barking was coming from behind a high wall, in someone's garden, and relaxed a bit.

His mother proved to have been a bit optimistic about what sort of food the village shop would sell, but he did his best. At least he got milk, and mousetrap cheddar and plastic ham for sandwiches. Anyway, it meant they'd have to go into St Andrews to shop this afternoon, which would break up the day a bit.

As he headed back towards the cottages, he wondered if perhaps he *could* cut through the fields. There were tall plants growing in rows. If he walked along between the rows surely he wouldn't be doing any harm?

He looked up and down the road. There was no one in sight. He stepped into the field and started along the nearest row. He'd only gone about twenty metres when there was an eruption of barking and the biggest dog he'd ever seen shot out of the vegetation in front of him.

He froze, terrified. Even if he'd wanted to run he couldn't have. Every muscle in his body seemed to have seized up.

The dog stood its ground, barking furiously, tail waving, for what seemed an age, but could only have been about thirty seconds, before a door banged nearby and a girl's voice shouted.

"Luath! Stop that noise! Come here you stupid dog."

The dog bounded off towards a girl who had appeared in a doorway in the wall next to the field.

She and Jake stared at each other as the dog lunged

for her, rearing up to put its huge front paws on her shoulders. To Josh's amazement she pushed it away carelessly. "Oh get down Luath, you idiot. Be quiet! Get into the garden."

The dog slunk through the doorway, head down, whining. She pulled the door shut behind it and continued to stare at Josh.

"What are you doing?" she yelled.

Why had he ever thought this was a good idea? Scared half to death by some hell-hound and now being bawled at by some stroppy girl.

"I was taking a short cut to the cottages." He jerked his head to indicate where he meant.

She walked to the edge of the field. "You'll be in trouble if the farmer catches you in his potatoes."

So that was what they were.

"I'm not doing any harm." He began to make his way back towards the road.

"Doesn't matter. You can't go through a field." She walked along the edge to meet him as he emerged. "You ought to know that. You're lucky it was Luath who caught you."

"How come it's all right for him to be in there but not me?" he said angrily.

"He's a dog. He's not meant to know to stay out; you are."

She was a bit smaller than him, sharp-faced, with dark brown hair in an untidy braid. She wore a striped sweater gone to holes at the elbows and cuffs, and a filthy pair of jeans tucked into wellingtons. He didn't think he'd seen anyone in wellingtons since he was about eight.

"You should keep your dog under control," he said abruptly, trying to hide his fear under bluster.

She saw through it at once. "He wouldn't have hurt you. He wanted to play." She gave him a narrow look. "You're not used to dogs either, are you?"

He said nothing. How much more of idiot was he going to be made to feel?

She bent down to pick something up – a piece of paper which she read with interest. He realized it was his shopping list.

"Were you hoping to get all this at the village shop?"

He wanted to say it was none of her business, but he had a feeling she'd laugh at him if he did, so he just said, "Yeah."

"I bet you only got the milk and cheese and tomatoes."

He smiled in spite of himself. "No tomatoes, but there was ham."

"Come on. We can give you some of this. We've far too much."

He started to say no, thank you, but she'd turned on her heel and started towards the door in the wall. Bewildered, he followed her.

She shoved the door hard and it opened with a creak of protest. The barking started up again and Josh hung back.

"Luath! Shut up! On your bed, go on." She poked her head around the door. "It's okay. He's in the house now. He won't come out. George has shut the door."

His face must have looked as blank as his mind felt.

"George is my grandfather. He and my grandmother Rose own this place." She gestured round the garden, which he saw for the first time as he stepped through the door.

Although his and Anna's flat at home didn't have a garden, some of his friends did, but nothing like this. Mostly they had green-brown patches of grass, and borders with flowers or shrubs, while a few had decks or patios. His friend Calum had a little pond where the two of them used to catch the same tadpoles over and over in the spring. There hadn't been any tadpoles for a few years now, though.

This was nothing like any of those. Little winding paths of bark led between trees with leaves like outstretched hands, or hearts, or feathers. Flowers bloomed in beds among the trees and the air was heavy with scent. It felt warmer than it did outside the wall.

The girl led him along the paths and past a pond the size of a double bed, covered in white water lilies, towards a greenhouse where a man was working, carefully removing damaged leaves from some tiny plant with hairy silver-green leaves.

"George," she said, pushing the door open, "this is ..." She stopped. "What *is* your name?"

"Josh."

"This is Josh. Luath just tried to eat him on his way back from the shop."

Oh no. She was going to tell her grandfather about him being in the field.

"Can we give him some ..." She looked at the list. "... tomatoes, a cucumber, red pepper, garlic and parsley?"

"Certainly." He straightened from his work and looked round at Josh, and held out a hand to shake. "Pleased to meet you Josh. I see my rude granddaughter isn't going to introduce us properly. I'm George Ferguson."

"And I'm Callie – Callie Hall," said the girl, looking a bit shame-faced.

George sighed. "I sometimes think the dog's better brought up than you, Caroline. Let's go and get these things for Josh."

He dusted compost off his hands and led the way out of the greenhouse and in through the back door of the house. Callie followed, Josh bringing up the rear a bit nervously, in case Luath was about to spring from ambush. He followed them through a workshop that smelled of cut wood and through another door into a cool, dim larder. George and Callie bustled about putting things into a bag, while he stood there feeling like a lemon.

"There you go." Callie handed him a carrier bag. "Sorry about the dog." It was the first uncomplicated thing she'd said to him, he thought.

"Thanks," he said awkwardly. "It was my fault anyway. I shouldn't have been in the field." Callie smiled and put a finger to her lips. George, busy in the far corner, appeared not to have heard. "How much do I owe you?"

"Nothing. We've got far too much anyway."

"Why's that?"

"It always happens when you grow stuff."

"You grew all these yourself?"

"Yes." She was laughing at him again. "You make it sound like magic or something."

"Anyway, thanks very much. I'd better go – I'm late."

Callie saw him to the garden door and waved goodbye as he set off, up the road this time.

***

I have lived all my life in Pitmillie village, have never been more than ten miles from it except when Beatrix and Janet and I stepped down into the little boat and went ...

But I should tell this in order.

Beatrix Lang and Janet Corphat and I were always friends even though they were five years older than me. We saw the world alike you see, and not as others see it.

I knew what I was when I was twelve. For months I spoke to no one of it, not even Beatrix and Janet, afraid of what they might do. But Beatrix and Janet already knew, of course, for they had made the same discovery about themselves and had already seen it in me.

"You're afraid, Agnes," said Beatrix. "But you don't need to be; not with us, for we're all alike. We've been waiting for you to realize."

"You're a witch, like us," Janet said, smiling. "You'd have worked it out sooner if you weren't the first one in your family."

So, of course, we grew even closer after that, and careful too, to do nothing that would make others suspicious. And we never hurt anyone.

We never whistled up a storm when we were by the shore. Any Fife fisher child would have known what we were about anyway. Instead, we did what we could to cure cattle and sheep and help the crops, without drawing any notice to ourselves.

It was Beatrix that had the idea.

"Blaw the wind where it likes
There's bield about Pitmillie dykes"

It was a saying everyone knew. There was always shelter near Pitmillie. The worst weather always seemed to pass round it. There was an old legend that said there was a way into the Kingdom of Summer nearby, and a little of the endless summer was always leaking out, like honey from a comb; so when three years in a row the summers were bad and the harvest was poor and people went hungry in the winter, Beatrix began to think.

"What if we could find our way in?" she said one afternoon last spring, when we were drawing water together. "If we could bring back SOMETHING, just a wee bit of something from the Kingdom, don't you think it would make the weather better here, help the crops and the beasts?"

"And how would we find our way in?" I asked.

She frowned. "I don't know. I'm thinking on it."

And that was how we the three of us came to cast the spell on Midsummer Night, when it hardly got dark at all and the new moon was like a nail-paring in the sky. Janet and Beatrix had had their heads together about it for weeks, deciding how best to try to find the way in.

They made a tiny boat of birch bark, that could sit in the palm of your hand. They painted an eye on the prow, so that it would find its way, then we each pricked our thumbs with the tip of Janet's knife and let a drop of blood fall into the boat so that it would know us.

Beatrix had a long coil of white silk thread. She tied one end to the boat and the other to a trailing branch, so the boat would find its way home, then set it down on the water of the tiny stream that flowed through Pitmillie.

2. LUNCH

She'd known at once when she saw him white-faced among the potatoes that he wasn't local.

She hadn't been able to resist poking fun at him gently as he'd tried to cover up how scared he was of Luath. She didn't tell him, as she should have, that lots of people were a bit cautious with him because of his size, pretending complete surprise at his reaction instead.

He had longish brown hair that curled a bit at the ends, and weirdly pale brown eyes. He kept pushing his hair out of his eyes as he talked to her.

The shopping list had given her a chance to make up for being spiky with him, and she'd watched him from her window all the way along the road as he went back to the holiday cottages.

⁂

"You were a long time," said Anna.

Josh rolled his eyes. "The shop hardly had anything, then some enormous dog jumped out at me and the mad girl who owned it invited me into her grandfather's garden and gave me all this." He held out the second bag he was carrying.

She took it, baffled, and unpacked tomatoes, a

cucumber, two red peppers, a bulb of garlic with the withered green top still attached, and a jar of honey.

"I didn't know that was in there. They grew all the rest. Do you think they made this?"

"I shouldn't think so. Did you pay them? Tell me properly who they are."

He explained over their unexpectedly lavish lunch.

They went into St Andrews in the afternoon, to have a look round and do a big shopping. Apart from the supermarket, his mother dragged him to a butcher's shop in Market Street to buy haggis, although he protested that he didn't like it, and to Fisher and Donaldson's cake shop. He didn't protest about that; in fact, the only problem he had with it was what to choose. Really, what he wanted was one of everything.

"It's just the same as when I was a student," said Anna, almost drooling.

Eventually, they each decided to have a fudge doughnut and a ridiculously creamy cake called a Devon Slice. Josh was all for eating them there and then, but Anna wouldn't let him.

"You have to earn it first," she said, with an evil smile, and dragged him off to play putting on an unbelievably hilly course that she said was called the Himalayas, before heading back to Pitmillie.

Josh had pointed out Callie's house as they drove into town. Now, halfway through his fudge doughnut, he was surprised as his mother slowed the car and parked outside.

"Why are you stopping?"

"I just want to say thank you for all that stuff."

"I already did that."

"I know, but I'd like to say thanks as well. Are you coming, or do you want to stay in the car?"

Josh swallowed the last of the doughnut and got out of the car with a sigh to follow his mother.

They went in by the front gate of the garden this time. Josh was not reassured to see a "Beware of the Dog" sign, but his mother paid it no attention, went up the path to the front door and rang the bell.

Josh had only seen the back of the house that morning. The front was like a child's drawing, all symmetrical four-paned windows and a central door. There was a deep pink rose climbing up the wall, and carved into the lintel above the front door was the date 1672. On the door itself was a sign that said 'The Smithy.'

There was a sound of footsteps inside the house in response to the bell and the front door was opened by a woman Josh had never seen before, but who he guessed must be Callie's grandmother. She had grey hair done up in a knot at the back of her head and bright, brown eyes. Looking at her, Anna thought she had one of those faces that would still look lovely in extreme old age, with clear skin and wonderful bones.

"Yes, can I help you?" she said, looking at them quizzically.

"I just came to say thank you. It was very kind of you to give my son the vegetables and honey this morning."

Comprehension dawned in the woman's eyes. "Ah, Josh and his mother, you must be. You're more than welcome; we've always got more than we can eat. It's good to be able to get rid of some of it.

"I'd call Callie, Josh, but I'm afraid she's out with George and the dog."

"Oh yes," said his mum. "I heard about this huge dog."

Josh cringed.

"He is big – a bit daunting if you don't know him. He's a Scottish Deerhound; we've kept them for years. Clever dogs, amazing vision. There's an old legend about them you know: that their eyesight's so keen they can see the wind." She seemed to fall into a reverie for a few seconds, then roused herself. "Why don't you come for lunch tomorrow? You can meet the dog properly and see where we grow the fruit and veg. It would be nice to have the company – especially for Callie. Don't ever say I said this but I think she gets a bit lonely for company her own age with just us old fogeys around."

Oh no, thought Josh. *Just say no, mum. Come on.*

"I'm afraid I'll have to say no. I'm up here to work – trying to meet a deadline for a book I'm working on – and if I start doing enjoyable things I'll never get it done."

Nice one mum.

"I'm sure Josh would love to come though." *What?* "I'm sure he'll be bored hanging around all the time on his own." *Nooooo!* "You'd like to come, wouldn't you Josh?"

He made some sort of *Urk* noise, which his mother decided meant, yes, I'd love to, and before he could do anything about it, he'd been well and truly *lunched.*

Back in the car, he turned on his mother. "Why on earth did you say I'd go? I don't want to have lunch with a mad girl and a couple of pensioners."

"First, it was very good of Mrs Ferguson to ask. Second, they were kind to you this morning, and if their granddaughter *is* lonely, it would be kind to go. Third, it gets you out from under my feet for another couple of hours."

"Charming. I don't know why you didn't just leave me at home with a week's supply of microwave pizza."

She didn't rise to it.

***

It was raining again the next day, but at least it was a bit warmer. Josh swam again in the morning and hoped his mother had forgotten about his unwanted lunch appointment, but at twelve thirty, she said,

"You'd better get ready soon."

He sighed, defeated, and went to get ready with the minimum possible effort.

Callie opened the door with a scowl on her face and her hand on Luath's collar. She looked as pleased to see him as he was to see her.

"This wasn't my idea," she said.

"Nor mine."

"Come in." She pulled the dog out of the way, just enough to let him squeeze past.

Don't react, he thought. *She's doing it on purpose to try and make you panic.* He managed to stroke the dog's huge grey head briefly as he passed.

"Outside, Luath." She pushed the dog into the garden and shut the front door behind him.

Josh followed her through into a kitchen with a big

wooden table in the middle. Pots were bubbling on the cooker and Rose Ferguson was slicing tomatoes.

"Hello Josh. It's very good of you to give up your time to join us."

"Thank you for the invitation," he said.

A silence developed awkwardly. Rose seemed quite unaware of it, or at least, unwilling to break it.

"Do you want a drink?" Callie said at last, and Josh thought he saw the corner of Rose's mouth twitch.

"Not just now, thanks."

"Callie, lunch will be another fifteen minutes. Take Josh across and show him round and bring your grandfather back with you."

"Okay. Come on Josh."

It would have been hard for her to sound less enthusiastic, but she led him out of the kitchen, stopping in the porch to pull on an ancient pair of trainers.

To his surprise they went out of the garden and across the road. About fifty metres ahead there was a white-painted door in the high wall that bordered the pavement. Callie shoved it open with her shoulder and Josh found himself in another garden.

This one was quite different from the one around the house. It was filled with straight rows of plants – vegetables, Josh supposed, though he had only a hazy idea of what most of them were.

Callie rattled off a list as they went past, but he didn't take much of it in. They came to a sort of tunnel made of metal hoops and thick polythene. "The interesting stuff's in here," Callie said, forgetting to sound bored.

Inside, she pointed out sweetcorn, a lemon tree, a grape vine, peaches – even a fig tree.

"I didn't think you could grow any of that stuff in Britain," said Josh, gently stroking a small, furry peach.

"You couldn't in most places, but we get better weather than most places. You still couldn't do it without the polytunnel though. Come on, I'll show you the rest."

The garden was packed with edible plants. Apple trees were trained against the walls. There was a walk-in cage of netting to protect the raspberries and strawberries that grew inside. Against one wall were two beehives, something that Josh had never seen in his life.

He edged cautiously closer, watching the bees come and go. "This is where that jar of honey you gave us came from?"

"Yes. A few people round here used to keep them, but these are the last hives in the village. The weather killed the rest of them, I suppose."

The farthest end of the garden was fenced off, and behind the fence a dozen black chickens wandered among another set of apple trees, pecking for insects.

"And this is where the cider comes from," said Callie, "and the eggs, obviously."

George was in there too, nailing a piece of wood onto the hen house.

"Lunch is nearly ready, George. Rose said to bring you back."

"All right," he called.

"Do you always call them by their names?" Josh asked.

"Of course. That's what they're called."

"I mean, you don't call them grandma or ..."

"No, I never have. They've always been George and Rose."

Since she was being relatively friendly, he asked the question that had been puzzling him. "Do you live with them all the time?"

Callie waited for him to step out of the garden onto the pavement, then pulled the door shut behind him. "No. My parents are doctors. They usually work in the hospital in Dundee, but they're in Ghana for six months doing voluntary work on an immunization project, so I'm staying with George and Rose while they're away. We live in the village anyway, so it's not very different from usual, except that they aren't here." Her voice had gone a little bleak as she spoke.

"What about you?" she asked

He shrugged. "Nothing to tell. My mum and me live in Edinburgh. She writes books on architecture; churches, mostly."

"No dad?"

He shook his head. "He's never been around."

"Do you mind?"

"Not really. I'm used to it being just mum and me."

They went back into the house, the ice between them thawing now.

"I thought you were bringing George back with you?" said Rose accusingly.

"He's just coming."

Everything they ate for lunch seemed to be home made: crab tart, salad and bread – even the ice cream that went with the strawberries. Josh couldn't remember eating a meal where everything tasted so good.

When they'd finished, George said, "Do you think your mum's in a hurry to get you back, or do you want to come for a walk down at Fife Ness with us?"

"She won't mind. What's Fife Ness?"

"Just a beach," said Callie.

"Not *just* a beach," corrected George. "The easternmost point in Fife. You get some good birds there."

"He's a birdwatcher," explained Callie. "Never goes anywhere without his binoculars."

George smiled. "Well, you never know what you might miss if you don't have them on you. Right, we'll just clear up, then we'll go."

⁂

They went in the car to Fife Ness, bouncing over the potholes for the last mile of unkempt road, past an abandoned World War Two aerodrome.

George went off on his own among the scrub and bushes, his binoculars ready round his neck. Callie and Josh made their way down to the beach, talking about their respective homes and schools.

She went to school in St Andrews, travelling in by bus every morning.

"Are there other people from the village who go there?"

Callie screwed her face up. "Yeah, but we don't exactly get on. They think I'm weird because I'm not into clothes and makeup and music and boys, and I think they're stupid because they are."

She probably didn't hesitate to tell them either, thought Josh. Just then, rain came without warning, rushing in from the east on a blustery wind. They were soaked in seconds.

"Come on, this way," yelled Callie over the drumming of raindrops. "I know where we can shelter."

They ran pell-mell, jumping boulders and piles of seaweed, trying not to slip on the treacherous slabs of rock. Josh was going so fast he missed the moment when Callie turned off the beach.

"In here, Josh!"

He slid to a halt and looked round to see Callie disappearing inside an opening in the rock face just behind the beach. He doubled back and followed her in, and for a moment they stood just inside, looking out at the rain and catching their breath, then Callie raked in her pocket and produced a tiny torch. She fumbled with the switch for a few seconds before she got it to work.

"Come on. Have a look round since we're in here."

She swept the beam of the torch around. The light from the entrance reached about five metres in, but the torchlight showed that the cave went further back than that.

She shone the torch at some vague circular shapes on the floor near the front of the cave.

"What's that?"

"George says it's a forge from the Iron Age, where they used to melt the iron out of the ore."

Josh whistled. "How old does that make it?"

"Oh, I don't know. Two thousand years? Three thousand? George can tell you all about it if you really want to know. He's got a bit of a thing about blacksmiths. I suppose it comes from living in a smithy."

"Come again?"

"Part of the house used to be the village smithy, long ago. I'll show you next time you're there." Abruptly, she swung the torch to point at the roof of the cave. "There are meant to be animals carved into the rock up there. I've looked and looked, but I can't see anything that looks like an animal. Can you?"

Josh squinted up as she moved the light across the rock. He couldn't see any animals either.

"There are lots of crosses cut into the back wall that you can see at least." She moved the torch beam to show him. "There are all sorts of legends about this place: that it was a magic forge, or a hiding place for monks, or that a king called Constantine was murdered here by the Danish Sea Wolves. That's where it gets its name – Constantine's Cave."

Callie was tracing some of the crosses in the wall with her fingers. Josh could see that a narrow passage led on from the back of the cave.

"How far back does it go?"

"Only a few more feet," said Callie dismissively. "It's not very interesting. Here, take the torch and have a look."

***

As we watched the boat it seemed to shiver, and then to swell like an oat in water, until it lay swaying gently,

a small boat still, but big enough for the three of us, tethered to a branch by a glimmering white rope.

Beatrix and Janet and I stepped down into the little boat, its silvery-brown hull stained dark red in three places, and sat. The stream seemed to have swollen as well. Normally you could step across it, but now it seemed to be six feet across or more, cut deep within its banks.

"We've no oars," I said. "How do we row?"

"Wait," said Janet.

After a moment, the boat began to drift downstream, but as though it moved with purpose. The white rope uncoiled behind us as we moved. Trees leaned in above us, their branches closing in until we slid through a leafy tunnel, green and silver and then green and gold as the sky above and before us changed and the tunnel of branches was bathed in sunlight, not moonshine.

The water flowed smoothly now, as though it was deep, and was clotted with plants. We drifted through them, speechless, struck dumb by a combination of fear and wonder at what we had done.

I never knew if we were in the boat for hours or minutes. In the Kingdom of Summer, time seemed to forget what to do.

At last, or perhaps after a few minutes, the stream widened to a still pool starred with white lilies, and the boat stopped at a little jetty of silvery wood that pushed out into the water. There was not a living creature to be seen: no man or woman, not even the song of a bird or the buzz of an insect among the branches.

We looked at each other.

"We must get out now," Beatrix whispered, but the silence that she broke was so perfect that we all winced at the sound of her voice.

We climbed carefully out onto the jetty. "Wait here," said Janet to the boat as we set off along a winding path of short grass that twisted away in front of us through the trees.

3. ICE

Josh edged carefully into the passage. The torchlight reflected back at him oddly from the walls, and it was suddenly very cold. He put out a hand to touch the rock. It was icy, and wet under his fingers, and when he shone the torch at the floor there was water pooled under his shoes.

"You didn't say it was wet back here," he yelled over his shoulder.

"It isn't usually. The rain must be coming in somewhere."

That made no sense. It was a passageway worn out of solid rock. He edged forward a bit further and came to an abrupt halt, the torchlight flashing back at his face. Cautiously, he reached out a hand to what blocked his way.

Ice.

He swung the torch beam up and down. The way forward was completely blocked by a wall of ice, smooth as a mirror except in one place, where a spur of rock poked through at about shoulder height. Disconcerted, he backed out into the main chamber, aware of the rise in temperature as soon as he emerged.

"What?" Callie was looking at him enquiringly. "What is it?"

"The ice. Is it always like that?"

"Ice? What are you talking about?"

"Look for yourself." He handed her the torch and she disappeared into the passageway.

A couple of minutes later she re-emerged, looking puzzled.

"That's totally weird. I've never seen that before. It's not even cold enough for there to be ice." She glanced at her watch. "George should be finished by now. Maybe he'll know why it's like that."

"Can I have another look?"

"Sure." She passed him the torch. This time, he shone the light at the roof, looking for signs of water leaching in, but the stone above his head was dry. He turned the light to the ice at the end of the passageway.

"What the ..." he muttered, moving closer.

The spur of rock that had been poking through the smooth surface of the ice was now no more than an egg-sized bump.

The ice was growing.

As he was about to call Callie, he heard her shouting. "George – come here! There's something strange in the cave." He looked over his shoulder and saw her silhouetted against the bright halo of the entrance. When he turned back, the piece of rock he'd been looking at was barely visible any more.

Moving the light across the ice, he was again about to call to Callie when something made him gasp and jump backwards. His elbow hit the wall hard and the torch fell from his tingling fingers and went out.

With a yelp, he scrambled backwards from the passage

into the main chamber of the cave and stumbled out and on to the beach. As he did so, he blundered into Callie, George beside her.

"Josh? What's wrong?"

"I ... nothing. I dropped your torch; I'm sorry. I think the ice is getting thicker."

Callie gave him a strange look, but said nothing.

"Let's have a look then," said George, pulling his car keys from his pocket. Josh wondered what he was doing until he saw a little torch like Callie's attached to it. He strode into the cave.

Callie turned to follow him. "Are you coming?"

"In a minute. I just want some fresh air."

She gave him another funny look, then followed George. Left alone on the beach, Josh listened to his heart slow down to something like normal.

He ought to go back in.

His feet didn't seem to want to take him.

Come on. You're being stupid.

He forced himself into the mouth of the cave just as Callie stepped from the passageway.

"The torch is fine," she said, waving it. "I think you're right about the ice," she wrinkled her nose, "but I don't understand how it can be doing that."

"Very interesting," said George, emerging behind her. "I've never seen that before, or heard of such a thing. We'll ask Rose, Callie. She knows lots of things that I don't. We'd best be getting back now anyway. I'll take you round to the cottage Josh."

The rain had gone off. As they walked back along the beach towards the car Callie looked sidelong at Josh.

"Are you all right? You were really pale when you came out of the cave and bumped into me."

"I'm fine. I bashed my elbow really hard on a rock when I dropped the torch. That must be why I was pale," he lied.

She didn't look convinced.

He couldn't tell her the truth. She'd think he was off his head. He couldn't tell her what had frightened him so much that he'd dropped the torch, because obviously she and George hadn't seen it, so obviously he'd imagined it.

Obviously. But it still seemed real. He'd shone the torch across the ice, and for a moment, he'd seen a man's face behind it, watching him.

***

Rose listened intently to George and Callie's description of the mysterious ice in the cave, brows drawn together in concentration.

"What do you think, Rose?" said George.

She dusted flour off her hands. "It all sounds very interesting."

"But what do you think could be causing it?" asked Callie.

"Causing it? I've got no idea."

Later, when they were eating their soup at tea time, Rose said suddenly, "George, did I remember to tell you I'm meeting the girls for coffee tomorrow?"

"I don't believe you did, my dear. Or perhaps I just forgot. Usual time?"

"Yes. Pass the bread please Callie."

⁂

All that evening, the image of what he'd seen in the cave drifted through Josh's mind, and he could do nothing to dislodge it.

"I got a lot done today," said Anna. "I think I'll give myself tomorrow morning off. We'll go into St Andrews and do something. I take it lunch wasn't as bad as you expected?"

"No. Callie's okay when you get talking to her. And I hardly saw the dog."

"Told you."

"I hate it when you say that."

"I know."

⁂

Unobserved by anyone now, the ice advanced to the end of the narrow passage then beyond, hour by hour, inch by inch, until the moonlight gleamed off a great slab of ice that filled the cave mouth. A trickle of water came from it and sank immediately into the sand.

As the night wore on, the trickle of water continued and the ice slowly receded, retreating back to the passageway, leaving behind in the centre of the outer chamber what it had carried with it.

A man.

Curled on the floor, icy and soaked, barely breathing, hair darkened by water, his hands clawed into the sand as if to hold himself to the earth, so that the ice could not carry him back again.

After some time he gathered the strength to raise his head.

"Come back," he whispered.

Come back.

The words floated into the middle of Josh's dreams. Fast asleep, he saw the face of the ice-man. *Come back,* he said, and Josh woke with a jump, his heart pounding.

It was frosty the next morning, white tips to every leaf and blade of grass.

"Frost in July!" said Anna. "This would never have happened when I was young."

They drove down the long hill towards St Andrews, a skyline of towers and spires, the sea shining on their right, steel blue.

"I bet that's cold," she went on.

"Mmnnn ... I'll stick to the pool thanks."

They found a parking space near Janetta's ice cream shop.

"Come on. Let's go up St Rule's Tower." She pointed to a tall, square tower beside the ruined cathedral.

"Why?"

"It's a great view from the top. Come on, you'll like it once you're up."

"It's the getting up I don't fancy."

"My son, the couch potato."

In the West Port Café, Rose Ferguson sat at a table with three other women about her own age, admiring a new hat one of them had just bought.

"It's lovely, Bessie," she said, "but tell me – why do you need *another* new hat?"

Bessie Dunlop smoothed the scarlet feathers around the crown and shrugged. "I just like to buy them. Then I know I'll always have the right one if I'm invited anywhere fancy."

Isobel Adam brought four chocolate biscuits out of her bag and handed them out, rather surreptitiously, to the others. "I don't know who you think is going to invite the likes of *us* anywhere fancy enough to wear that!" she said mildly.

Bessie sniffed dismissively and put the hat back in its box. "Speak for yourself dear. At least *I'll* be ready. I might go on an exotic holiday like Barbara does and have to dress for dinner."

"I've never had to wear a hat for dinner," said Barbara Napier, "I don't know anywhere *that* exotic!"

"Anyway, that's enough about hats and holidays. Rose, when you asked us to meet here yesterday, you said it was important. What's going on?"

They all turned to Rose, attentive and serious now.

"Girls, I think things are coming to a crisis." She told them what George and Callie had seen in Constantine's Cave.

"Do they have any idea what it means?" asked Barbara.

"George has an inkling, though even he has no idea how bad things would be if this really is the start of the Black Winter rising. Callie ..." She shook her head. "We must find a way to put this right. We've all seen how the weather is changing and how the changes are speeding up. We *must* find a way."

Isobel put a hand on her arm. "I know my dear, but haven't we been trying for years already? What can we do that we haven't done before?"

They fell silent.

⁂

Josh was relieved to hear his mum breathing harder than him as he came out behind her into the cold sky at the top of the tower. He looked round.

There was a solid looking wooden barrier to keep anyone from getting right to the edge.

"Huh! When I was a student you could sit right on the edge if you wanted to. Blooming health and safety people! Anyway, they can't take away the view. I told you it was worth it."

Even Josh was impressed. On one side the sea, gleaming like sheet-metal; the town spread like a quilt around the base of the tower, and beyond, farmland and hills to the edge of vision, all silver-chilled with the last of the frost.

He leaned as far as he could over the wooden rail.

"Didn't anyone fall off when you could sit on the edge?"

"Not as far as I know. I mean, it was pretty obvious you'd to be careful not to lean too far back. They had to watch out for drunken students of course, but they just didn't let them up. It seemed to work."

Josh was looking at the landscape below them again.

"It's frostier that way than it is down towards the village."

She screwed up her eyes against the sun and the frost glitter to see better. "Yes, you're right. Maybe because we're nearer the sea. I think I remember reading that keeps the land warmer. I mean, you hardly ever get snow right down by the shore anywhere in Scotland, even now."

Josh remembered the ice in Constantine's Cave and wondered about that. A voice said in his ear, "Come back." Startled, he whipped round, half-expecting to see the man from the ice, but there was no one on the tower besides the two of them. He gave a shudder, the hair standing up on the back of his neck.

"It's freezing up here. Let's go down." He shivered.

"All right."

Now that the ice-man was back in his head, he wouldn't leave Josh alone, the face in his memory, the words unavoidable. He *must* have imagined it, but he could still remember the shock of fear when he saw the face. He had to go back to the cave. That was the only way he'd be able to get rid of this feeling that he couldn't put a name to.

They went for hot chocolate, then shopped for food. As they drove back to the cottage Josh said tentatively, "I might see if Callie wants to do something this afternoon, if that's okay." Anything to derail his imagination.

"Of course. Why don't you invite her over for a swim or something?"

"Yeah, might do. You can drop me at her house as we go past, then I'll walk up to the cottage."

"Are you all right?"

"Yes, of course. What do you mean?"

"Offering to walk. That's not like you."

"Must be the country air or something."

⁂

Callie came to the door with a tortoiseshell kitten climbing up her sweater.

"There's no one else in," she said. "Just me and Chutney Mary, not even Luath." She turned and went inside, leaving him to follow.

"Chutney Mary?"

She detached the kitten from her chest and held it out to Josh. "This is Chutney Mary."

"Why?"

"Well, she has to be called something and George and Rose don't seem to think Come-here-you-stupid-cat is good enough."

The kitten was trying to chew his thumb off. "Ouch. I never knew their teeth were so sharp. Isn't Chutney Mary a bit of a ... weird name?"

"Probably no weirder than any other name seems if you're a cat."

There didn't seem to be an answer to that.

"What do you want anyway?"

"I wondered if you wanted to come over to the cottages, if you're not doing anything. We could have a swim, or watch a film or play pool or something. Only if you've nothing better to do of course."

Why did he always feel such a prat when he talked to her?

To his surprise she looked delighted. "Can I come with you now? I'm bored out of my mind."

"Eh ... yeah. Of course."

"Hang on, I'll just shut Chutney Mary away so she doesn't shred all the curtains."

She disappeared with the kitten and reappeared a moment later with a heavy jacket over her fraying sweater. "Right," she said. "Let's go."

⁂

Bathed in golden light, we followed the path through groves of oak and birch and rowan, and other trees that we did not recognize. The sun cast rippling patterns of light and shade on the bark and at our feet, as a breeze moved the leaves above us.

We moved, speechless, as though we were caught in a dream. Perhaps we were.

The path rose steadily. We walked one behind the other, Beatrix in front. She stopped suddenly, and Janet and I caught up to her and together we looked out from the edge of the wood.

Below us was a grassy valley, smooth as a bowl, wide and shallow. It seemed to catch all the light in the sky and throw it back. And at its centre, like the pupil of an eye, was a building such as we'd never imagined, much less seen.

Its walls were not of stone or brick or daub and wattle, but of living wood. The white trunks of birch trees, slender as dancers, were linked and coiled about with great stems of roses and honeysuckle. It was a palace: one that had grown, not been built. Arched doorways pierced walls of leaf and blossom, but there were no doors to bar our way and still no sign of anyone.

We stood on the edge of the wood, appalled now by our

effrontery. I tugged at Beatrix's sleeve, to say "Let's go back," but as I did so, a Kingfisher flew out of the wood behind us and swooped down and in through one of the windows.

As it did so, the spell of silence that seemed to bind the place was broken and we became aware of the plash of water, the noise of insects, birdsong and voices from within the palace.

Before we could move forward or back, a woman walked out through the main doorway. She stopped just outside, looked up to where we were and smiled.

"Come down," she called, "since you have found your way into my Kingdom."

Clinging to each other, we began to make our way down the grassy slope. She walked towards us. Her feet were bare, and where they touched the grass, tiny flowers of white and gold sprung up in her footprints. Trembling, we walked to meet her and when we drew near, sank to our knees before her, not daring to look up.

"Why have you come here?" she asked, and then we had to look up at her in all her fearful beauty.

Her ageless face was full of wisdom as well as loveliness. Poets would write verses, but I cannot, so here is the best I can remember: eyes the blue of a summer night, lips like poppies, hair to her waist that seemed like petals and oats and sunlight and streamers of high cloud. Her dress was a gauzy thing of shifting patterns, green and blue and chestnut, like a butterfly's wing or a Kingfisher's feathers, traced over and over with rippling veins of gold.

We had found the Queen of Summer.

4. CONSTANTINE'S CAVE

Although she had lived in Pitmillie all her life, Callie had never been to East Neuk Cottages before, which seemed strange when they were so near, or so Josh thought.

She was fascinated by the place, by what seemed to her the enormous choice of things to do. In the pool, she spent ages just floating on her back, staring happily at the roof as Josh swam and dived around her.

"This is the warmest pool I've ever been in," she announced, by way of explanation. "Mostly I swim in the sea."

Josh spluttered. "You're joking! Here? It must be freezing."

She turned and disappeared below the surface, sleek as a seal in her tatty old black costume. Josh had never met anyone with such a total lack of interest in what they wore. She'd have been bullied mercilessly at his school. He was ashamed to realize that he would probably have joined in.

But here, she was so confident that she made it seem as though everyone else who fussed about brands and labels was mad and she was the sane one. He wondered what happened to her at school in St Andrews.

After they'd swum Callie persuaded him to go for a walk. It didn't take much persuasion, since he'd been looking for a chance to ask about going back to Constantine's Cave.

"I've never walked round here before," she said. "It's weird now I think of it. I suppose I've always thought of it as somewhere that's only for the people staying in the Cottages; but I don't suppose it is."

They had wandered along a path between drystone walls that marked the edges of fields, and were now cutting across an area that had been planted with row on row of trees. There must be thousands, thought Josh, and even he knew that they were proper trees, not grotty forestry plantation conifers. Not that he could have put a name to any of them, mind you.

They were back on a narrow grassy path now, behind a thin screen of taller trees. Suddenly Callie stopped him with a hand on his arm, a finger to her lips. She pointed through the trees. Josh looked and saw three deer grazing in the adjacent field, quite close, oblivious to their presence. He'd never seen wild deer before and he watched them for several minutes. Then he must have moved without realizing, and their heads swung up together and they raced off.

"Well, I would guess that you haven't seen anything like that before?"

He shook his head, not rising to the bait, and walked on.

A bit further on was the ruin of a cottage, half obscured. They ducked through the doorway. It smelled of damp, and of old wood, and after a few minutes they shoved their way out through the ivy again and cut back towards the Cottages by the side of a tiny stream, almost hidden between its overgrown banks and overhung by bushes and small trees.

"If you're not busy tomorrow," Josh said at last, "is there any chance we could go back to that cave and see what's happened to the ice?"

"George and Rose are going to Dundee in the car to see some sort of exhibition. Can you cycle?"

"Yeah, of course."

"You could borrow my dad's bike and helmet." They were nearly back at the Cottages now. "Come round at ten. Shall I bring a picnic?"

"Yeah, that'd be good – only if it's not raining, mind you."

"Wimp!"

❋❋❋

A cold rain set in again that evening, dying away as darkness fell and the frost returned. In The Smithy Chutney Mary slept curled on the pillow among Callie's hair, and Josh burrowed down under the duvet up the road at East Neuk Cottages.

In Constantine's Cave the man lay huddled at the back of the cave, his eyes closed, picturing a little stream clotted with weeds, and a palace of briars, and a woman whose face he saw now only in his dreams.

At the edge of the shore near Pitmillie the water turned thick and slow, moving less and less.

The sea froze.

Something dragged itself, cracking, from the sea ice, and lumbered up onto the beach, shedding weed and sand and shells as it moved inland.

Luath's barking woke everyone in the house. George and Callie stumbled from their bedrooms, Callie with the kitten clamped to her shoulder in a state of terror. Rose pushed past them, wide awake, and went at once to where the dog stood trembling, hackles up, behind the front door. Without hesitation she opened it.

"Rose – don't! It could be a burglar," called Callie. George said nothing. A gust of freezing air that smelled of salt and weed blew in, rattling the loose window in the kitchen. Luath stopped barking and edged into the dark garden, growling.

"What do you see, dog?" muttered Rose under her breath. She could sense nothing. "Is it the wind? Is that what you see? Or is there more?"

Even in darkness every shape looked familiar. Luath trotted around it a few times, his agitation diminishing, then shook himself, came back in and lay down on his bed.

"I reckon the dog had a nightmare," said Rose to no one in particular.

"Do dogs have nightmares?" asked George.

"This one does." She shut and locked the door, muttering quietly to herself. "Well, we may as well get back to bed. Goodnight."

But it was a long time before any of them slept.

As Josh walked round to Callie's next morning, he could

see his breath hanging in the air like smoke. He wore jeans and a long sleeved tee shirt, a hoodie and his fleece jacket. It he'd had gloves he'd have worn them too. He wriggled his toes in his trainers to keep them warm.

As he pushed open the gate he saw two muddy mountain bikes propped in the garage, good ones by the look of it. Unlike the bikes he and his mates rode in town, these both looked as if they might have been up a few proper hills.

Something crunched under his feet as he went up the path to the front door. He looked down to find a scatter of weed and shells and sand round his feet.

He rang the bell and heard Luath barking somewhere inside. He was getting a bit more used to him now, but he didn't think he was ever going to turn into a dog person.

Callie came to the door yawning.

"Am I too early?"

"No." She swallowed another yawn. "I just slept badly. Luath was having nightmares or something. He woke us all up barking at something in the garden."

"What was it?"

"Nothing, as far as we could see." She focused on the sea-wrack round his feet and frowned. "Was that you?"

"No. What – do you think I brought a bucket of seaweed with me to tip over your garden?"

"Sorry; no, of course not. I just wondered where it came from. Come in. It's cold, isn't it? I was just getting some food for us."

Josh followed her into the kitchen, where George was reading the newspaper, an enormous mug of tea in one hand.

"Morning," he said. "Hope you've got your thermal underwear on. Mind you, the cycling will warm you up."

Callie was putting packages of what Josh hoped was food into a small rucsac, while the kitten chased dust balls across the kitchen floor.

"Hello Josh, dear," said Rose, absently going through the kitchen without stopping. "Ten minutes, George."

"Yes, my dear."

✽✽✽

"Come on Luath. Out we go." Rose opened the front door and the dog bounded into the garden, tongue lolling. Rose shut the door behind her and took a crunching step along the path. She stopped, looking down, and her hand went to her mouth.

"Oh no," she whispered. "Oh please, not yet." The dog pushed his head against her leg. "Oh Luath, you felt it come, didn't you?" She stroked him absently. "What are we to do? What are we to do?"

✽✽✽

It wasn't very hilly between the village and the coast, for a good job. Josh was used to cycling of course, but not really to cycling so far in one go.

At least he wasn't cold, although the frost seemed to get heavier the further they went from Pitmillie.

They came into Crail and turned along the road to Balcomie. A little later they passed Balcomie Castle sitting in the middle of its farm, and then there was only the golf course between them and the sea.

Now that they were here, Josh wasn't sure that he wanted to be. The whole episode with the face behind the ice seemed almost like a dream. He wished he could convince himself that was what it had been, but he couldn't. He knew that he had to go back to the cave before the thing would resolve itself, but he was happy to put it off when Callie suggested they go for a walk in the little wood on the hill.

"There's normally lots of birds in here," she said. "I don't know why it's so quiet in here today. Of course, they've done really badly raising young in the past few years." She seemed to assume he would know what she was talking about, so he nodded in agreement.

It was definitely colder here than in the village. There was even a skin of ice on the little pond they passed on their way back down to the beach.

"How about some food?" he said. "I'm starving. Must be all that cycling."

Callie shrugged. "Okay." She doubled back along a narrow path that ended at a bench that gave a view down the hill to the chilly sea. She took off her back pack, sat down and started rummage. "Cheese all right?" She passed him a roll crammed with salad and a thick slab of cheese. "There's coffee in the flask. Help yourself."

"Thanks." He munched his way slowly through the roll. He wasn't actually that hungry. It was just a way to put off going back to the cave.

The coffee was no longer very hot, but it washed down the cheese roll well enough. He turned down the offer of a flapjack for the time being.

"Let's go and look at that cave again, see what's happened to all the ice."

"Righto," she said, round a mouthful of roll. "Just let me finish this."

They walked along the path at the edge of the golf course this time instead of on the beach. There were a few birds here, down by the shore, standing on rocks or pecking at things in the sand. Josh wondered what they were. He was pretty sure Callie would know, but he didn't want to ask her. He was getting fed up of being the one who didn't know stuff.

They rounded a corner and the rock face with its cave was in view. Right, time to set his mind at rest.

The grasses and bushes round the foot of the rocky outcrop were crisp with frost, and it crackled under their feet as they left the path and made their way towards the tall, arched opening.

His heart beating hard, Josh stepped round and into the cave mouth, Callie just behind him. He forced himself to look slowly round the cave, trying not to think about going into the narrow opening at the back.

He almost stopped breathing.

There was a figure sitting on the ground in one of the shallow recesses at the back of the cave, head on folded arms on drawn up knees. Josh knew what his face would look like.

He wanted to run, but his muscles wouldn't do anything. Callie moved round him, apparently unconcerned, saying, "Hello. Are you all right?"

The man didn't move.

"What do you think we should do?" Callie whispered,

turning to Josh. She caught sight of his face. "What is it? What's wrong?"

He managed to speak.

"The ice. I saw him before in the ice."

"Josh, you're not making any sense. What do you mean?"

The man still hadn't stirred.

"When we were in the cave before and there was all that ice in there –" he gestured at the narrow opening at the back of the cave "– when I went back to look again there was a man's face behind the ice. That's what made me drop the torch."

They were speaking in whispers now.

Callie gave Josh a long, hard look, but to his amazement, not only did she not laugh at him, she seemed to take his ridiculous statement seriously.

"But in that case he'd have to be dead, wouldn't he? He doesn't look dead. And how could George and I not see him?"

"I don't know. I know it doesn't make any sense. What are you doing?" Callie was edging towards the still figure. "Come back!" he hissed. "You don't know what he is."

"Well, he's not dead, whatever he is. I can see him breathing."

"Leave him. Come on, let's get away from here."

"No! What if he's ill, or hurt?" She kept sidling closer.

"Hello," she said quietly. "Can you hear me? Are you all right?"

There was no reaction from the huddled figure. She said it again, more loudly this time. Still nothing.

Josh moved closer.

The man was dressed in clothes made from what

looked like animal skins, soft and supple, dyed blue and grey. He could see the stitching at the seams on the sleeves. They were decorated with patterns of coloured thread and pieces of shell and what looked like bone. His hair was a mix of black and various greys, longer than Josh's. There were small braids through it, with pieces of bone and silver and fragments of blue feather woven into them.

As he watched, the pattern of the man's breathing changed. Josh began to back away, but before he got more than a few feet the stranger lifted his head and fixed his gaze on Josh. His eyes, as he had known they would be, were a piercing light grey, and his face was filled with melancholy, but when he saw Josh, a sad smile spread slowly across it.

"I knew you would come," he said.

⁂

"Come," she said, and turned and led us to her hall, and we followed as though we were spellbound, and I suppose we were.

The air was full of the scent of flowers and honey and green things growing.

We walked in under a lintel of living wood into a breathing palace that had no roof but the open sky. Still we clung to each other's hands as we followed the Queen over a carpet of flower-starred grass to a white birch that had shaped itself into a throne. I could hear voices here and there, but still saw no one, but now birds and butterflies and dragonflies came fluttering through the windows, and suddenly, where there had been no one there were men, tall and fair, with long, clever eyes, and women so beautiful I could not look at them.

The Queen seated herself on her throne, soft as a drifting leaf. "Now, tell me why you have come to my Kingdom."

As usual, it was Beatrix who found her voice. She told the Queen how the crops had come close to failing for the last two years, and how cold and wet the weather had become, told her of the winter hunger we had come to dread, how the Laird claimed his share – a third of the harvest – even when we had hardly anything.

"And so we have come to you," she finished, "to ask for your help. We thought that maybe, if you would let us take back something from here, we might take the summer with us, and maybe we could make the weather better for the crops and help the folk."

The Queen sat, considering. Near her, a young man changed into a dragonfly and flew away.

"What do they call you, in your village, that would dare such a thing as this?"

"They'd call us witches if they knew; and then they'd kill us," said Janet.

"Foolish folk they must be, to turn on those who would help them."

"The church tells them they should. They're feared they'll go to hell if they don't follow its teachings."

The Queen laughed. "Poor souls, to live in such fear and ignorance. Very well then; let us see if we can help them." She thought for a moment, then called over a woman whose plum-coloured hair hung, curling, to her hips. She said something to her that we did not hear. The woman smiled and then she was a swallow, fluttering out of the nearest window.

"Will you take food and drink with us while you wait?" asked the Queen, and men bearing trays of pale polished wood set them down at her feet. There were bowls of summer berries and soft white bread and honey and cups of golden liquid.

I would have taken a cup and drunk, but Beatrix kept my hand pressed in hers and said, "We thank you for your hospitality, but we may not eat in your Kingdom or likely we will never come back to our own."

The Queen locked gazed with her for a few seconds, then smiled and said: "As you wish."

At that moment, the woman with plum-coloured hair reappeared. She carried a tiny crystal phial, which she handed to the Queen. The Queen took the stopper out and held it up so that the sun flashed off the cut facets; then she stoppered it again and held it out to Beatrix.

"What's in it?" Janet asked. "It looks empty."

"It is full of air from my Kingdom."

"Air? Will that help us?"

Beatrix's hand tightened on mine and I felt myself grow cold. Janet's tongue could bring trouble anywhere. The Queen however, merely smiled at her ignorance.

"In you world it will be very ... potent. Open the phial in your village and you will see."

We muttered our thanks.

"We should go back to our own world now," said Beatrix.

"Yes," said the Queen, nodding, "for who knows how much time may have passed while you have been here?"

Her words sent a chill through my heart and I saw it reflected on the others' faces as we exchanged fearful looks. We got to our feet slowly.

"Thank you for helping us, Majesty," said Beatrix, Janet and I repeating her words like an echo. The Queen of Summer waved her hand to dismiss us and it was obvious that she had already lost interest in our small concerns. It seemed clear we were to leave.

We walked slowly across the fragrant flowering grass to the doorway and paused to look back.

There was no one to be seen in the great hall of the palace, in human form at least. Here and there butterflies danced among the flowers, and there was a flash of blue as a Kingfisher took flight.

We quickened our pace once we left the palace, feeling the Kingdom grow wilder about us, as though the Queen's concentration had moved elsewhere. We looked back at the palace once more from the edge of the wood, then set off down the path through the trees, anxious now, hearing her words in our heads. WHO KNOWS HOW MUCH TIME MAY HAVE PASSED WHILE YOU HAVE BEEN HERE?

Silence closed in about us again as though the wood waited for something, its breath hushed. We dared not speak.

I remember that my legs shook with relief when we came down to the lily-strewn pool and the silvery jetty and saw the boat still there. Carefully, we climbed into it as quickly as we could. A Kingfisher feather floated on the water beside me and I picked it up, for a keepsake.

Janet pushed us away into the middle of the pool.

"Take us home, little boat," she said and sure enough the boat began to drift, going upstream this time, without oars or sail, pushing between trails of water weed under the gold-green tunnel of trees, under the silver-green tunnel of trees, the sky darkening until the clearest thing to our eyes was the glimmering white rope stretching away ahead of us.

The trees opened out and we came to where the rope was tethered to a branch. Wide-eyed, we stared at each other. Beatrix opened her hand and there was the crystal phial, safe and solid.

"What if years have passed in Pitmillie? What if no one knows us? Or what if we suddenly become old when we set foot on true soil again?"

"Look around you, you silly fool. It's all the same as when we got into the boat: same trees, same bushes. Look at the moon: it's hardly moved in all the time we've been gone. If anything, time has run quicker in her Kingdom than here." Beatrix sounded exasperated and exhausted.

I had no choice but to believe her, but all the same, as I set my foot on the earth of the river bank I screwed my eyes tight shut for fear that I should see my own foot crumble to bones and dust.

Beatrix got out with her precious cargo, then Janet. She untied the rope from the branch and dropped it into the boat.. The boat slid away from the bank and drifted away back down the stream.

"It wants to go back," said Janet. "It is her thing now."

We watched it out of sight.

5. The Winter King

"I knew you would come," he said.

Josh stood very still.

"What does he mean, Josh?" Callie said beside him.

"I don't know," Josh lied.

"I dreamed about you," said the man, "and in my dream, I called you. *Come back,* I said. I saw you through the ice, as I forced myself here. You saw me." By his side, Josh heard Callie take in a quick, sharp breath. "Yours was the only face I knew, and I saw your face in my dreams and I called you. *Come back.* And you have come."

Josh didn't know what to think or say or do. He hoped he was having a nightmare. He tried to think of the relief he'd feel when he woke, but somehow he didn't think this *was* a dream. What he mostly wanted to do was turn and run away from this strange man, but his legs seemed to have forgotten what to do. Besides, there was Callie.

She'd shown no sign of fear – in fact nothing but naked curiosity since they'd come into the cave. He looked at her now, saw her wide-eyed gaze flicking between their two faces.

"Who are you?" she said. Josh hadn't even had the wit to ask.

"I am the Winter King."

"Where are you from? Why are you here?"

He said nothing for a few moments. Instead he got stiffly to his feet and walked to the cave mouth to look out. He was a head taller than Josh, and strongly built, his greying hair hanging to his shoulders. In the brighter light at the entrance they could see how intricate were the patterns dyed and embroidered into his clothing.

He looked at the grey sea out of his grey eyes, and Josh thought he had never seen a sadder face. Grief seemed frozen into it.

"Here. Careful – it's hot." To Josh's surprise Callie handed the man a cup of coffee. He sniffed it before he drank, then sipped, eyes closed, concentrating on it as though it was something precious, until he'd finished every drop. There was a trace of colour in his pale face now.

"Thank you. What was that?"

"Coffee." Callie touched his hand as he held the cup out to her. It was icy cold. "Would you like some more?"

He shook his head. "That is enough for now. I feel warmer than I have in ..." He left the sentence unfinished, turned back into the cave and sat down again.

"I do not know your names."

They told him and he nodded, committing them to memory.

"Where are you from?" Callie asked again.

"I have come from the Frozen Lands, where there are no trees, not a blade of grass, nothing but fields of snow and rivers of white ice and seas of blue ice, and white gulls crying."

"Do you mean you're from the Arctic somewhere?"

Josh asked, though it sounded stupid to him even before the words had properly left his lips.

"No," said the King. "It is no place that you know of."

"Are you hungry?" asked Callie.

"Yes."

She held out a leftover cheese roll to him. He nodded thanks and began to eat.

"Let's go. He's mad," Josh muttered to Callie.

"Don't you want to hear what he has to say about calling you? He seems harmless anyway."

"No, I don't want to – and you don't know he's harmless. You don't know anything about him," he hissed.

"That's why I want to listen to him. You go if you want, I'm staying. I was taught not to run away from things."

The final comment made Josh so furious that he was lost for words for a few seconds. When speech returned, it was to the King he spoke.

"Why did you call me?"

"I need help. I am grown too weak. I have waited too long."

"What sort of help? Too long for what?"

"How much can you believe?"

Josh let himself slide down the rock wall opposite the man who called himself the Winter King until they both sat, facing each other. He felt, rather than saw Callie settle at his side.

"I don't know. Tell us your story and we'll see."

He nodded and closed his eyes. There was silence for such a long time that Josh and Callie began to think he must have fallen asleep again, but eventually he began to speak.

"I have not seen her for so long. Sometimes I fear that I dreamed her face; but it is the memory of that face that made me keep trying to put right the wrong that has been done.

"I speak of the Queen of Summer, for the Winter King is chosen by her as her champion and her Consort, to hold the Black Winter through her power within the Frozen Lands. Together we subdued the forces of Winter, held back the ice and snow when they threatened the fragile folk of this world. She held the power of the sun in her two hands and conjured summer to force back the cold. In the Kingdom of Summer no snow fell or cold wind blew, and such was our strength together that for half the year I could leave the cold white lands and live with her."

He shifted slightly. "And then she began to sicken and her power began to wane and I had to leave her side for longer and longer to subdue the Winterbringers, and each time I returned to her she was a little weaker, her Kingdom grown a little colder. At first she tried to pretend that nothing was wrong, but her people knew; I knew. Some of her power, some of herself, had been stolen away, out of her Kingdom, and without it she was doomed to sicken and die."

He straightened his shoulders as though to face a confrontation, and went on, "After a time I realized that my presence weakened her faster. At first it seemed that it would be enough if we no longer touched, and so we bore that, but after a time I could see that even to be near her drove the cold a little deeper into her bones, into her heart. I could not bear the thought that I was hastening her death, and so one morning I left her and went back to the Frozen Lands for good. I have not seen her face since."

Silence spread over the cave floor. Josh had no idea what he was supposed to make of the fantastic story he had just heard, but he found himself unable to dismiss it as easily as good sense suggested he should. It tugged at something within him.

"How long is it since you saw her?" Callie asked quietly.

He thought. "Time is different for you and me, but as far as I can reckon it, it is a hundred and fifty years."

It seemed no madder than anything else they'd heard since they entered the cave.

"Why have you come here?" asked Josh. "And why now?"

"Because she is dying, and I cannot bear to be apart from her any longer, and it would not help her now if I stayed in the Frozen Lands. I weaken day by day as her power withers. The only thing that could save her now is if what was stolen from her was returned, and what hope is there for that? Her Kingdom is almost sealed now, but this is the place where the Frozen Lands and the Kingdom of Summer come close enough to almost touch and I believe there will still be a way through for me. I will go to her when I sense that it is time and be with her when she dies, and then the Winterbringers will have their way: the Black Winter will come and the ice will stretch away forever."

"What do you mean? Just in your ... Frozen Lands? Or do you mean here?" asked Josh, suddenly worried that he understood.

"Everywhere. Everywhere. It has already begun."

"Is that why it's been getting colder?"

"Yes. Though here it is less bad than in other places."

"I know. Everyone in the village notices, but no one knows why," said Callie.

"They say it's Global Warming that's made it colder. Something about shifting the Gulf Stream. But it's supposed to get hotter in other places. The ice at the poles is meant to melt," said Josh.

The Winter King shook his head slowly. "You people tell stories about everything to try and make sense of what happens. That story is wrong. The ice will spread until it covers everything, as it has done in the past as the power of each Winter King waxed and waned."

"There's more than one of you?" Callie frowned, confused.

He shook his head. "No. The Queen is ageless, but not her people. Her Consorts age and their powers weaken until the Winterbringers overwhelm them. That is when the ice spreads into your world until she chooses a new Winter King. He must prove himself by forcing the Winterbringers back to the Frozen Lands. So the powers of Winter and Summer waxed and waned, but there was always balance."

"The ice spreading ... you're talking about the Ice Ages, aren't you?" Callie asked.

He nodded. "But without the Queen there will be no end to this one. Nothing but rivers of white ice and seas of blue ice ..."

Josh asked the question that had been nagging at him. "If there is nothing that can help, why did you call me?"

"Because it is you who saw me in the ice. You anchor me to this place now. Without you I cannot stay here. As I grow weaker I will be drawn back to the Frozen Lands and overwhelmed. If you are close, my strength will last longer. I called you so you would know.

"There is another reason too: to be a witness. So that there is someone who knows the truth and will tell it and set it against all the false stories. It will take time for the ice to win. Your people will fight it and try to explain it with stories, but this is the truth of it."

"Prove it." Callie's voice cut in, cool and assured. "Prove you're what you claim and not some madman in fancy dress."

The Winter King held her gaze and Josh found himself holding back words. *How can you look at him and doubt him? Look at his face. Look into his eyes. However unbelievable his story seems, look and you must see it's true.* Perhaps that's another reason why he called me, he thought.

"As you wish," said the King. "I will let in a little of what I hold at bay." He closed his eyes, and snow began to fall in the cave, a few flakes at first, like swansdown, then coming faster and faster, though Josh could see that there was no snow beyond the cave mouth.

As she turned towards the rear of the cave watching the flakes fall, Callie saw something shiver and form in the air at the dark entrance to the ice passage. It was like looking down the wrong end of a telescope: she was looking at a miniature but extraordinarily clear view of a landscape such as she had never imagined.

Blue and green and white and glittering, ice stretched

past the limits of her sight, smooth or jagged or carved into wild shapes by a ceaseless, screaming wind. There was not a tree, nor blade of grass, nor inch of earth; nothing and no one but white gulls crying in the fierce air.

It hurt her eyes to look at it, but she found she couldn't turn away.

"Josh?" she whispered.

"I see it," he said quietly.

The snow whirled around them now, a miniature blizzard, each flake a tiny, stinging slap of cold. It clogged Josh's lashes and ran down his neck. It was bitterly cold.

"Enough! Stop!" yelled Callie's voice from somewhere inside the storm of white. The flakes still in the air settled and were still and Callie and the King faced each other.

"All right," she said shivering, "I believe you."

Snow was sifted into every crevice of the cave, and lay thick on the ground. It stopped at the entrance as though cut by a knife. Outside, a watery sun still shone.

"There must be something we can do – some way we can help *you* at least."

He hesitated. "It would help me if you came back again. You are my anchor to this place. Your presence will strengthen my hold here."

"You could come back to the village with us. You could stay in my family's house; there's no one there just ..."

"No. Thank you. I must stay here as long as possible. From here I have most power over the Winterbringers. You must come back here."

Come back. Come back.

"Of course. At least, I will," Josh said, shivering.

"We both will," Callie said firmly.

"But now you must go. Close your doors and windows after dark, for the ice ranges further each night."

They didn't understand exactly what he meant, but chilled and confused as they were, they were easily persuaded to go.

Josh paused at the boundary between the snow and the outside world. "We'll be back."

"I know."

⁂

In the West Port Café, Rose and her friends sat at their usual table, their coffee and scones untouched in front of them. No one had spoken for nearly five minutes; a thing unheard of. In the middle of the table sat a honey jar, half full of sand and weed and fragments of shell. They all stared at it glumly.

"What does George say about all this?" asked Isobel.

Rose sighed. "You know George: he doesn't really say anything. He guesses some of it of course, but not how bad things are, or how much worse they could get."

"Did you see the ..." Bessie gestured, looking for a word that would do.

"No," said Rose as Barbara lifted the jar and unscrewed the lid to sniff the contents. "The dog woke. He knew there was something outside, though not what, or I doubt he'd have been so keen to get out beside it."

"We must try again to conjure a proper summer," said Barbara, putting the lid back on.

"Sshh!" hissed Isobel. "People will think we're mad old women if they hear you saying things like that."

"They'll have more to worry about than other people's conversations soon if we don't manage to do something," retorted Barbara darkly.

"We must do it tonight," cut in Rose. "We can't wait any longer."

"The tower?" asked Bessie.

Rose nodded. "At moonrise. You all know what to bring?"

They nodded and fell silent again.

"Does anyone want my scone?" asked Isobel. "I'm not really hungry any more."

***

When my mother shook me awake the next morning I thought for a few seconds that I'd dreamed the whole thing; then I saw the Kingfisher feather I'd tucked in among the daisies in the little jug on the windowsill, and every detail came back at me clear and sharp.

I ate my porridge without even sitting down, my mother's acid comments about my laziness buzzing about my ears like stray bees, then went to my chores absent minded, waiting for the evening, when we'd meet again and find what we had really brought back with us.

It was a strange day. The air seemed heavy and still and quiet to me, as though some sort of blanket lay muffling the whole of the village. It was as though a thunderstorm were brewing, but there wasn't even a wisp of cloud to be seen for most of the day.

That evening I made some excuse to leave the house and walked out over the fields to the place where we'd set the boat afloat the night before. Beatrix and Janet were already there, flushed and bright-eyed with excitement, the way I felt myself.

We looked about for a minute to be sure no one was watching us, then Beatrix took the phial out of her apron. We passed it between us, watching the evening sunlight glance off the smooth, shining faces. It looked quite empty.

I handed it back to Beatrix. She glanced at Janet, then at me.

"Now?"

We nodded.

Biting her lip in concentration, she twisted the glass stopper. It moved smoothly in her fingers. She paused for a heartbeat, then pulled it gently free.

A warm breeze sprung from the bottle, fragrant with honey and roses and summer rain. It swirled around us, moving the grass and shaking the leaves on the trees. Round and round us it traced a widening spiral until the crops and grasses and twigs were moving everywhere. Then it dropped away to nothing, leaving a fugitive scent of honey.

Beatrix put the stopper carefully back in the bottle, her hands shaking a little as she did so.

"Well," she said, "that's that."

"Wait," said Janet, pointing to a little group of trees across the corner of the field. "There's someone there."

Sure enough, a figure came darting out, running towards the village. I peered into the thickening light, trying to make out who it was, and was relieved when I did.

"Ach, it's only that fool of an apprentice of my father's, Patrick Morton."

Janet grinned and tutted, shaking her head in feigned disapproval. "Has he been following you again, Agnes? You know he wants to court you, don't you?"

I spat on the ground. "I wouldn't have the idiot if he came in a gold box."

Beatrix cut in. "Be serious you two! Do you think he saw anything?"

"What was there to see?" said Janet dismissively. "Three women talking and a wee bottle with nothing in it."

Beatrix looked worried. "All the same. Be nice to him for a bit Agnes, just in case. You never know what'll set folk's tongues wagging. We must be careful." She handed me the phial. "You keep this. If he asks, show it to him, so he can see it's nothing strange. Tell him we found it by the stream."

"All right." I tucked it in my pocket.

"Maybe we should stay away from each other for a bit ... just in case," Beatrix went on, still looking worried.

"Maybe you're right," said Janet, standing and stretching. "At any rate, we should be getting back. It'll soon be dark."

It was a good harvest – more than good: the best anyone could remember. Since midsummer the weather had been warm and the sun had shone and enough rain had fallen when it was needed; and when the harvest came in, everyone was happy, for it meant that this winter at least, no one would go hungry. As Beatrix had suggested, we stayed away from each other, her and Janet and me, but when we met by chance we couldn't

help but catch each other's eyes and smile, as folk talked of the full barns and storehouses.

I let Patrick Morton put his arm around my waist and follow me around and talk to me, but he was still an idiot, so I slapped his face when he tried to kiss me. It didn't put him off though, more's the pity.

Maybe that's why ... maybe it was my fault. Or maybe it was his hand on my waist that has saved me this far.

6. Send the Summer In

After they had gone, and the snow on the cave floor had melted, he stood at the entrance to the cave and watched the sky. It was a calm evening, the waves running gently up the shingle in front of him. Already, he could see the crystals of frost beginning to form on the clumps of grass and scrubby bushes just outside. When the dark came, he retreated inside and sat down against the back wall. He closed his eyes and gathered his waning strength to oppose the forces of Winter.

Josh was astonished to realize it was still only mid afternoon when they got back to the Ferguson house. He felt exhausted; not just from the unaccustomed long distance cycling, but from their strange encounter in the cave and all the anxiety that had been building up inside him for the last couple of days. He felt he was on the edge of something that might change his life forever, sweep away everything he thought of as fixed and certain.

Callie was silent as they wheeled the bikes into the garage and put the helmets away. "Do you have time to come in?" she asked as she shut the garage door.

He nodded.

Luath rose from his blanket filled basket as they came through the front door, making a sort of grumble that wasn't quite a growl. Callie scratched his head absently as she went in. Josh hardly noticed him, then realized he hadn't and was so surprised that he stopped and dared to stroke him. Luath's tail banged against his legs in pleasure.

They went through to the kitchen and Callie unpacked the remains of the picnic, while Josh teased Chutney Mary with a teaspoon.

"It makes sense you know." Callie spoke without preamble.

"What does?"

"What he said about the ice coming. You just have to think how cold it's been over the last few days, and how the weather's changed during the last few years. Global Warming? Huh! Even in George and Rose's garden there are fewer and fewer things that will grow each year."

"It's got hotter some places – look at the droughts in Africa – look at what it's like where your parents are."

"But that's only temporary. The whole of Northern Europe's getting colder, not just Britain; and the weather's gone crazy everywhere: droughts and hurricanes and mudslides and ice storms and people dying of heatstroke. It's all out of control."

"If you believe what he says."

She turned and looked at him properly. "It's hard not to, when you talk to him. You do, don't you?"

Josh nodded. "I do. I saw him in the ice. I know he's more than a madman."

"But there's nothing we can do?"

"He said there wasn't. I can't even imagine anything we could do, can you?"

She shook her head.

* * *

George and Rose got back about five, shortly after Josh had crunched off through the frost back to East Neuk Cottages.

"How was the exhibition?" Callie asked them.

"Oh, very interesting. Lots of things in boxes," said George, bafflingly.

Rose seemed unusually preoccupied, moving around the kitchen automatically, putting together a meal.

Callie watched her for a few minutes. "Are you all right Rose?"

She looked round, her eyes caught somewhere far away for a second, then smiled, her mind coming back to the kitchen. "Yes, of course dear. Just thinking about all the things I saw today.

"I think we'll eat early, shall we? I have to go into St Andrews for a while after supper."

"What for?"

"Oh, nothing really. I promised Barbara I'd help her with some ... baking."

Callie gave Rose a puzzled look, but her expression in return was quite blank.

Although they had turned up all the heating in the cottage to full, it wasn't very warm. Anna turned on the television as they ate their pasta and they watched news reports about the record low temperatures for the time of year.

"Some summer holiday I've brought you on," said Anna.

"It doesn't sound as though it would have been much better anywhere else – unless you prefer somewhere that's burning up in a drought."

They watched the weather forecast in glum silence: hard frost for the next few nights and even a suggestion that it might snow in some areas.

⁂

Rose drove carefully through the dying light down the long hill into St Andrews, going over the situation in her head for the hundredth time. She parked the car near the Cathedral and got out, a shapeless figure muffled in layers of fleece topped off with an old duffel coat, a knitted hat pulled down hard round her ears. She reached back in for her basket and shut and locked the car door, looking round. At this time of year the streets used to be lively with tourists up for the golf or a family holiday, but tonight there were only two heavily dressed figures hurrying through the frost-sharpened air towards the refuge of home.

She checked that no one was watching, spoke to the gate in the wall around the Cathedral grounds and walked quickly through it when it swung open.

Ahead of her there were already sets of footprints cut

into the frosty grass leading towards St Rule's Tower. She followed them and found the narrow door at the bottom ajar.

Inside, Barbara and Isobel stood, muffled as she was against the weather, each carrying bags. They waited in silence for the five minutes until Bessie arrived. She was wearing her new hat.

"You're late!" hissed Barbara.

"I am not," retorted Bessie indignantly. "The moon's not up yet."

"And what on earth are you wearing *that* for?"

"I might not get another chance. Anyway ..."

"Never mind about that," Isobel cut in. "Let's get on."

They began to climb the narrow staircase, saving their breath for the moment. A few minutes later, they emerged, panting, onto the open platform at the top of the tower, where Josh and Anna had stood the day before.

It was darker than it should have been for the middle of August, a great mass of grey cloud off to the west smothering the last of the sun's light. The evening star burned wanly, low in the sky to the south.

They busied themselves with preparations as they waited for the moon to rise, unpacking an odd assortment of bits and pieces from their various bags and baskets.

Isobel produced an elderly and blackened wok, and proceeded to build a sort of nest of small twigs inside it. Rose brought a jar containing a piece of honeycomb out of her basket and set it down nearby, as Bessie carefully unwrapped a rose cut fresh from her garden, dark red, newly opened from the bud, the edges of its petals blackened and crimped by the frost.

Barbara's bag contained a little garland of woven grass, a handspan across, the grass braided in an intricate pattern. Lastly, Isobel reached into a pocket and shook a single long feather out of an envelope.

"How long have you had that put aside?" asked Rose.

"Five years. That's the last time I saw a swallow. I've another two still, laid away safe at home."

"Are we ready?" Barbara said, stamping her cold feet. The others nodded. "Then let's light the candles."

They stood as the moon rose, one on each side of the square platform of the tower, facing in towards the things they had brought with them. Each of them held a candle. Rose's was in the shape of a Santa Claus, the wick sticking out of the top of his hat.

The others looked at her.

"It was the only one I could find!" she protested. George has tidied them all away somewhere, and I was in a hurry. Anyway, you know very well it doesn't matter what the candle looks like."

There was a second of silence, then the four of them burst into laughter, a welcome release of the tension they all felt.

"Let's light the candles," repeated Barbara.

Each of the women held a candle in her left hand and cupped her right hand over the wick. When they took their right hands away, the candles burned steadily, Bessie's with a red flame, Isobel's blue, Barbara's green and Rose's golden.

They bent down and pushed the bases of the candles into the network of twigs in the wok. The candle flames spread as the twigs caught, crackling, and the coloured flames ran towards each other and joined and mixed, until the whole bowl was filled with hot, white fire.

They joined hands and Rose began to speak.

"Queen of Summer! Queen of Summer! Hear our plea. Far from the Kingdom of Summer we call to you. Summer has bled from these lands; has fled from these lands. The Winterbringers are abroad, and all the land will soon be locked in ice. Hear our plea, Queen of Summer. Send the summer in. Send the summer in. Send the summer in."

They let go of each other's hands and Isobel stepped forwards and bent to pick up the Swallow tail feather. She dropped it into the fire, where it lay untouched by the flames around it.

"Send the summer in, Queen of Summer. Send the swallows back to tell us summer has returned."

Isobel was replaced by Barbara, who tossed the garland of grass into the flames to join the feather.

"Send the summer in, Queen of Summer. Send the sun to ripen the hay."

Bessie stepped forward next. She sniffed at the rose before she let it fall into the fire.

"Send the summer in, Queen of Summer. Send the flowers to feed the bees."

Last of all, Rose came forward. She tipped the jar up, and the piece of honeycomb slid out and fell into the wok. The four objects they had brought lay untouched within the white fire.

"Send the summer in, Queen of Summer. Send back the bees, the keepers of memory, the memory of summer locked in each comb."

The fire blazed up, sudden and fierce, consuming what had been fed to it. The chilled air around them warmed, and scents of roses and hay and honey wrapped them round. They turned now to face outwards and linked hands again and spoke all together.

"Queen of Summer! Queen of Summer! Hear our plea. Send the summer in. Send the summer in. Send the summer in."

Fire shot upwards in a towering white column that only they could see, then broke like a wave and poured down the sides of the tower and rolled away from it across the town and the countryside in all directions.

The four women stood on top of the tower, eyes closed, hands linked. The fire they had conjured died away to nothing and there was just an old black wok, some burned twigs and the twisted remains of four candles.

Rose gave a great sigh. They let go of each other's hands and turned inwards again.

"Well, we have done all that we can," Rose said.

"But I wonder if it's enough?" mused Bessie, bending to pick up her bag.

"We'll know by the morning," said Rose, half to herself.

They collected their bits and pieces and came slowly down the tower stairs. At the gate that led back onto the street they separated to go back to their own homes. Rose got into the car and drove very slowly back to the village, too tired to dare go any faster.

When she came into the kitchen, George looked up, trying to read her expression.

"Did everything go all right?"

She shrugged. "It seemed to, but who knows? There's nothing more we could have done anyway.

Where's Callie?"

"In her room. She's in a funny mood. Do you think she senses ...?"

"I shouldn't think so. More likely to be something Josh has said to her I should think."

"Do you want anything?"

"No. I just want to go to bed. Will you make sure everything's locked up?"

"Of course."

"George – I mean *everything.*"

"Don't worry, I'll do it properly."

***

The night wore on. In the Ferguson house Callie and Chutney Mary slept twisted together; George snored beside a sleepless Rose, and Luath dozed fitfully, head on his paws, tantalizing traces of scent troubling his sleep.

At East Neuk Cottages, Josh and Anna slept burrowed under downies and extra blankets, trying to escape the cold.

In Constantine's Cave the Winter King sat against the cold stone, his arms wrapped round his chest, concentrating all his strength on forcing back the cold. Something had quelled it for a time earlier, but now he could feel it once more, struggling to break free of his control. He knew he did not have the strength to keep it at bay for much longer.

But he had to try.

❦❦❦

By Pitmillie beach, the sea slowed and thickened and glazed with ice. It clotted and bulged, groaning and cracking with its own life as two figures hauled themselves from it.

They were vaguely like men, but like statues only half-shaped, the hands and feet unfinished, club-like, the faces nothing more than blurred suggestions.

They stepped from the sea ice and lifted their heads and sniffed and set off ponderously up the beach towards the village.

❦❦❦

At three in the morning Luath lifted his head from his paws and began to growl deep in his throat. Ears flat, he backed slowly away from the front door, the growl turning into a howl.

Within a minute George, Rose and Callie were all downstairs, Callie still half asleep.

"What is it? What's wrong?" she asked, rubbing her eyes.

"Nothing Callie. It's all right," said George.

There was a dragging sound outside the door and Luath edged further away from it.

"What's that?" Callie looked from George to Rose, alarmed now.

George made to lift the curtain over the hall window.

"No George – leave it be," Rose said sharply.

Callie turned to her. "What is it? There's someone out there. What's going on?"

"There's nothing," said Rose desperately.

"Of course there is," Callie almost shouted. "You know what's going on, don't you? Tell me!"

"All right: I will, I promise, but please not now."

The noise outside died away and Luath fell silent and moved cautiously towards the door, nose and ears twitching.

The three of them stood frozen to the spot as the smells of weed and water drifted in to them.

"Go back to bed Callie," said Rose, in a tone of voice that Callie had never heard before, one that she wouldn't have dared disobey.

When she went upstairs, George and Rose were still staring at the door.

In her room, she went at once to her window and moved the curtains just enough to be able to look outside. She could see no one in the dark garden below her, just the frost-rimmed shapes of shrubs and trees, but when she looked out over the potato field where she'd first seen Josh, she thought that near the far side she could see two figures, glimmering yet indistinct against the darkness.

She curled up tight in bed and left the light on.

***

Josh didn't know exactly what woke him, nor, at first, where he was. He poked his head out from under the covers for some air and to get his bearings and remembered everything at once, just as the noise came from outside his window.

He went rigid, trying not to breathe. *Don't be stupid,* he told himself. *Either you just imagined it, or it's the wind or a fox or something.*

He had just begun to relax when it came again; a scraping sound just outside his window, as though something heavy was being moved across the gravel.

He found that he could hardly breathe. Although he listened, there were no more sounds, but he couldn't shake the idea that something was outside.

Shamefaced, he crept from his bed through to his mother's room and shook her awake.

She couldn't remember how long it had been since he came to her frightened in the night. Looking at his face, she put aside the jocular things she'd been going to say, wondering at the same time why she wasn't frightened when he so clearly was.

They stood in his room, listening to nothing.

"It was probably a fox," she said, "but let's put on the outside light and look from the sitting room.

The sitting room had french doors and a switch for the outside spotlight. Josh hung back while his mother switched on the light and pulled back the curtains.

There was nothing to see.

The spotlight illuminated everything for a fair distance from the cottage, but all it showed was the stiff white outline of frosty plants.

They looked for a few seconds longer.

"Sorry," said Josh.

"That's all right. You must just have woken up from a dream and carried some of it over with you, or something like that."

He turned to go back to bed, but she spoke again. "Look!"

He followed her pointing finger. A few flakes of snow were beginning to fall.

***

Towards the end of October, Patrick Morton fell ill. I'd paid no attention to him the day before when he kept complaining of a headache as he worked at the forge, but that morning when I went past his house his mother called me in and told me he had taken to his bed and wanted to see me.

I went reluctantly, for I'd no wish to see him at all, and found him in his bed all right, tossing in a fever. I was about to creep away when he opened his eyes and caught at my arm.

"Agnes," he groaned. "Don't let them do this to me. You can stop them. I know you can.

"What are you talking about?" I said roughly, pulling my arm free. "You're ill. Go to sleep."

"They must have cursed me, those other two."

I felt my blood turn to ice.

"I don't know what you're talking about," I said, my voice thin in my own ears.

"Beatrix Lang and Janet Corphat – of course you know what I mean."

He caught my wrist again and pulled me down close to him, his eyes glittering with the fever. "I know about the three of you. I know YOU would never hurt me, so it must be the other two. They've cursed me to stop me speaking out about them."

"No, Patrick! How can you say such things? It's the fever speaking. Beatrix and Janet curse you? What nonsense! I don't know what you've imagined about us, but it only exists in your own head."

It was a marvel to me to hear my own voice so steady now, when my legs were shaking and I could feel the blood skittering through my veins.

His grip was strong in spite of the fever. I twisted my wrist this way and that, but I couldn't break free.

"Stop your lying Agnes. Have you forgotten I was there at mid-summer? I saw the three of you working a spell. I know you are a good woman: I won't ever give you away; but the others ... they should be tried."

I stared at him open-mouthed in horror, then with one last pull I managed to wrench my wrist free. "You're a sick man, Patrick. You don't know what you're saying."

I ran from the room to find Beatrix and Janet, to warn them. Everything conspired against me that day, but now I wonder what good it would have done anyway if I had managed to warn them. How were they to have escaped?

Between my chores that day I ran here and there around the village looking for Beatrix and Janet, but I never laid eyes on either of them, for they weren't in their homes and no one seemed to know where they were. I hoped that meant that they had fled before Patrick had a chance to denounce them, but I had a sick feeling in my stomach about them.

That evening, I called in at Patrick's house, hoping he'd have forgotten what he'd been raving about in the morning, but the fever still raged in him and when I went into the room his mother was there, listening to his rantings.

She gave me a look that was hard with suspicion. "I'm away to fetch the Minister," she said.

"He's not that ill, surely?" I was truly shocked.

"No. The Minister should hear what he's saying about these women."

I'd to grip the back of a nearby chair to stop my legs giving way under me. If Patrick denounced them to Minister Cowper they were as good as condemned, for he was fierce against witchcraft.

"I should go home," I muttered.

"Aye, I think you should."

I couldn't think what to do, terrified as I was for Beatrix and Janet, and for myself. I could leave the village, run away, but where could I go? There was no one in another place to take me in. I'd probably die of cold at the side of some road during the winter.

When I got home I told my mother that I didn't feel well – maybe I'd caught what Patrick had – got into bed and pulled the covers over my head. All night I lay awake, listening for the sound of folk coming to take me away, but there was nothing and just before dawn I must have finally fallen into an uneasy sleep.

In the morning I kept to my bed, trying to shut out the world. There was nothing I could do to help Beatrix and Janet now. All I could hope was that Patrick Morton hadn't repeated his accusations to Minister Cowper.

I ignored my mother's shouts to get up and pretended to be asleep when she came in, and to my surprise, she let me be.

About the middle of the day, there was a knock at the front door, and my heart seemed to turn to stone in my chest. For nearly half an hour I strained to catch scraps of conversation, but I could make nothing out. Then I heard the door close and my mother's footsteps coming towards the bedroom.

I jumped back into bed and pretended to be asleep again, but this time she did not leave. "Agnes, wake up. I must talk to you."

I yawned and stretched and opened my eyes; and then she told me that the Minister had had Beatrix and Janet arrested on suspicion of witchcraft and that they were to be interrogated later.

I don't remember much more of what she said, except for how ill I looked.

A little later she brought me up some broth. "Agnes," she said, "you used to spend a lot of time with those two. Did you ever think there was anything ...?" She let the question die away.

"Of course not. They're ordinary folk. Just like you and me."

❋❋❋

I will seal these papers and the things I brought from the Kingdom of Summer in my little strongbox and put them in my father's hidey-hole so that my family will know the truth one day; for if they do come for me, they'll surely let me speak to my mother or father before the end.

My name is Agnes Blair and every word that I have written is true, so help me God.

The twenty-ninth day of October, 1704.

7. The Smithy

Morning came.

Callie woke in her narrow bed. Something was different. The air sounded odd, hushed. She climbed out from under the downie and pulled a curtain aside to see a white world, everything dusted with a thin powdering of snow that seemed to muffle all the usual noises. The sky was pearl-white, clouded from horizon to horizon.

She thought of the Winter King in the cold cave on the sea shore and her heart sank.

The radiator creaked and gurgled as the central heating came on and she heard someone moving about in the kitchen. She pulled on some clothes and went downstairs, pushing her hair out of her eyes, Chutney Mary following her as though she was a dog, not a cat at all.

In the kitchen, Rose moved around automatically making breakfast, her mind blank with despair. They had brought their combined strength to bear on the cold last night, and it had no difference whatsoever. Their failure had been total. There was nothing else left for them to try.

It had been bad enough last night – already the ice creatures were abroad – but now it would get worse. And worse. And there would be no end to it.

She tried to rouse herself to be more normal as Callie came into the kitchen, yawning.

"Have you seen the snow?"

"Yes," said Rose, "and the sky looks as if there's more to come."

"What's going on with the weather?" said Callie, as though she didn't know.

Rose hesitated, tempted for a moment to tell her the truth; but what good would it do? It wouldn't help anyone. So she just shrugged her shoulders. "They say it's the Gulf Stream moving."

"Do you think that's it?" Callie pressed her.

"How would I know? I'm not a scientist. I suppose they know what they're talking about."

Callie sat down and started to butter toast. "You promised you'd explain about last night."

Rose turned briefly from frying bacon to give Callie what was meant to be a reassuring smile.

"I didn't want to worry you in the middle of the night."

Now we're getting somewhere, Callie thought.

"You know there have been sightings of Big Cats between here and Cupar over the last few months?"

Callie's baffled expression was unfeigned. Of course she knew about that – there had even been a sighting outside the secondary school in Cupar last spring – but why was Rose bringing it up now?

"I didn't tell you, but George saw it just up the road last week. Luath went after it into the trees then came running out with his tail between his legs." The bacon sizzled in the pan as Rose turned it. "From Luath's reaction last night, I think that must have been what was outside. That's why I didn't want to open the door.

Do you want some bacon?"

Callie shook her head and ate a mouthful of toast to give herself time to think.

Big Cats? What was all that about? Whatever she'd seen from her bedroom window certainly wasn't a Big Cat.

"You don't think last night was something to do with all this weird weather then?" she asked.

Rose turned round, frying pan in her hand, face expressionless. "I suppose it might be making the cat a bit ... bolder. You know, if it's having trouble finding food or something."

"That's not what I meant. There was ... I saw ... oh, never mind." Defeated, Callie returned to her toast.

❄❄❄

In the cave by the sea, a huddled figure lay on the floor, features glazed with ice, scarcely breathing, trying to will his strength across the miles, across the worlds, to Her.

❄❄❄

"This heating's hopeless," said Josh's mum, putting her hand against a lukewarm radiator. "Feel that – it's hardly warm at all." She turned the oven on and opened the door. "Let's see if that helps."

Josh buttered toast, saying nothing. As soon as he

got up, he had looked out of his window for any sign of whatever had been there last night, for he was still sure there had been something – but the snow was a blank white sheet.

"Put the TV on, will you?" Anna said as she made coffee.

He took his toast over to the sofa, curled up and switched it on to a breakfast news programme. It was full of reports about the freak weather and far from being an isolated local event, it seemed that the area around St Andrews had so far been spared the worst. There was footage of snowploughs in Edinburgh and London, and pictures of the sea frozen off Newcastle.

His mother sat down beside him. "Maybe we should go home," she said.

"No! I mean ... it looks worse there, not better. Anyway, it can't last, can it? Not at this time of year, surely?"

She sighed and shook her head. "I don't know, Josh. It shouldn't be happening at all. I don't know what's going on. I don't think anyone does, whatever they say."

There was a knock at the door and the owner of the cottages came in.

"Morning. Just to let you know we've closed the swimming pool for the moment. We can't get it to heat up at all in this weather and the last thing we want is to blow the wiring so that the heating in the houses goes off. Sorry, but I've never known anything like this. We'll let you know as soon as things get back to normal."

He crunched off to the next cottage.

"Well, that's swimming out, unless you fancy breaking

the ice. If you don't want to go home, what are you going to do?"

"I thought I'd go and see Callie for a bit."

His mother gave him an arch look. "You two seem to get on very well."

He sighed, trying not to show how annoyed he was. "It's not like that. We do get on – as friends, that's all."

"Okay, okay. Sorry I spoke."

He went into the bedroom to get dressed and when he came out she was already at work at the dining table, deep in a litter of papers.

"I'll be back for lunch. Do you want me to get anything from the village shop?"

"Some cheese – and eggs if they've got any. Thanks. Are you going to be warm enough?"

"Yeah. It's not far after all. See you."

"Bye."

The cold caught at him as soon as he stepped outside. Now he understood why the heating didn't seem to be doing much. He trudged off down the track, hands deep in his pockets, chin tucked down into his jacket as far as possible. It was like being underwater somehow, this fierce cold.

He'd intended to go to the shop first, but he was shivering so much by the time he reached the Ferguson house that he decided to go in there first for some respite.

As he walked up the path he noticed that the paint on the front door was scratched and gouged from top to bottom. He rang the bell and waited impatiently, stamping his feet, for someone to answer.

After a moment, Rose opened the door. She looked so surprised to see him that he wondered, belatedly, if he should have phoned first.

"What happened to your door?"

Her expression told him she didn't know what he meant until she looked around at the outside of the door he was holding open. Her eyes widened and her face turned pale.

"Did Luath do that?"

She shook her head. "No, not Luath ... it must have been the cat," she said, collecting herself.

"The cat? She couldn't have done that," Josh said, baffled, as he followed Rose inside.

In the kitchen he found Callie yawning over a cup of coffee, her hair even more of a mess than usual.

"It looks as though you slept even worse than me," he said.

"Huh. I bet you're right. The dog woke us all up at three in the morning barking at something outside."

"Was that when your front door got trashed?"

"Trashed? What are you talking about?"

"Haven't you seen it?"

He followed her back to the hall and watched her stare at the gouged door.

"Rose thinks it was the cat, but the cat couldn't have done all that."

Callie shivered. "I wanted to open the door and see what Luath was barking at, but Rose stopped me. I looked out of my bedroom window and I saw two ... figures ... going off over the fields. I was sure that Rose knew something about what was going on, but when I asked her this morning she started talking about Big Cat sightings. I don't understand at all."

"Ah ... *Big* Cats. I thought she meant the kitten." Callie rolled her eyes. "All this happened at about three o'clock, you say?"

"What?"

"The dog woke you at three o'clock?"

"That's right. Why?"

"Something woke me at about half past three." He cleared his throat. "I thought there was someone moving about outside my window. Or something. But when I looked, there was nothing there." He didn't mention having woken his mother. "Do you think that's just coincidence?"

She shook her head slowly. "But what do you think it was? Or who? You don't think it was the Winter King?"

"No. I'm sure it wasn't – he said he had to stay at the cave."

"We didn't imagine him, did we?"

"You know we didn't. Anyway, just look out of the window. This is what he said would happen."

Callie ran her fingers down the gouges in the front door. "These aren't even like claw marks," she said. "They're much too broad, more like fingers."

"I wouldn't like to meet whatever it is that has fingernails that can do that," said Josh, measuring his own hand against the marks.

Callie shuddered and pushed the door shut on the cold garden.

She looked around. "Puss, puss ... where have you gone?"

They looked around the kitchen, under the table,

under chairs, in the laundry basket, but there was no sign of Chutney Mary.

"I thought she usually stayed beside you?"

"She does. She follows me like a dog, not a cat at all. Puss ... where have you gone?"

"Maybe she's got into your bed to keep warm."

They went upstairs and searched Callie's bedroom, but Chutney Mary wasn't there either.

George and Rose joined in the search, but the kitten was nowhere to be found.

"She didn't get out while we were looking at the front door?"

"No, I'd have seen her."

They went back to the door anyway and looked outside, but there were no paw prints in the snow.

"Oh, she'll turn up," said Rose. "Cats do this all the time. They're nowhere at all, then suddenly they're sitting right in front of you, licking their paws and trying to look innocent."

"You don't suppose Luath ...?"

"Of course not," said George. "If he was going to eat her he'd have done it long before this. It's not as if we keep him hungry after all. Don't worry, she'll turn up as soon as you stop looking for her."

"Go and light the fire in the smithy, Callie, would you please?" asked Rose. "And I'll bet you she's sitting in the kitchen when you go back in."

Josh had never been in this part of the house before. It was a big, formal sitting room dominated by an enormous chimney. To one side of the hearth sat an anvil. He stared at it; he'd never seen one before.

"George found it buried under the floor when they put the central heating in," said Callie by way of explanation. "This used to be the village smithy. That's why it's got this huge fireplace."

She was holding an armful of logs, ready to pile them in the fireplace.

"Sshh!" said Josh.

"What?"

He held up his hand, and they both listened carefully. A thin mewing came from somewhere in the room.

"She's in here!"

"Sounds like it."

Callie put the logs down with a thud in the middle of the carpet. "Puss, puss, puss, where are you?"

They listened again. For a moment there was nothing, then the mewing started again, more insistent this time. They moved around the room, trying to find her.

"She's stuck somewhere," said Josh.

"The chimney! She's in the chimney." Callie stepped up onto the hearth and ducked her head to see under the chimney canopy. "I need a torch." Her voice emerged muffled. "It's too dark to see her. There should be one on top of the fridge."

"I'll get it."

He returned a minute later with the torch. The chimney was so big that Callie had been able to stand up in the fireplace, her head and shoulders disappearing under the canopy. He poked her in the back to get her attention and passed her the torch.

Indistinctly, he heard her talking to the cat, then

the torch clattered to the floor and she squirmed out covered in soot, clutching Chutney Mary, who was no longer tortoiseshell, but black from nose to tail.

"Take her for a minute, would you?" She thrust the filthy kitten into his arms, picked up the torch and disappeared into the chimney again. "There's something ..." Her voice died away to a mutter, then a shower of soot came down the chimney and she reappeared holding something black and about the size of a brick.

"What's that?"

"I don't know. It was wedged into a recess up the chimney. The cat was sitting on it when I found her. Is she okay?"

"I think so." He held the kitten up level with his face and she sneezed a little cloud of soot at him. "What do you want me to do with her?"

"We'll need to give her a bath. We'll use the kitchen sink."

They retreated from the smithy, trying not to get any more soot on the carpet.

It was amazing, Josh reflected as he looked around at the kitchen ten minutes later, how much mess bathing one small sooty kitten could create. Rose and George had left them to it and disappeared off to the garden across the road to tuck fleece round various plants that the cold was on the verge of killing. There were puddles of soapy water all over the floor, wet towels and of course, the outraged kitten, now backed into a corner and spitting, while Callie tried to tempt her out with a piece of cooked chicken.

He let the grimy water out of the sink and glanced out

of the window. It had begun to snow again, big leisurely flakes drifting down.

"She's fine now," said Callie. Chutney Mary sat demurely under a chair, damp fur sticking out in every direction, tail curled neatly round her paws, eating the piece of chicken. "I'm just going to get cleaned up. Why don't you make some coffee?"

"Okay."

Filling the kettle, he noticed that the snow was falling faster. He'd take a lift back to the cottage if it was offered.

He turned his attention to the object that Callie had pulled out of the chimney, which was sitting on a newspaper on the kitchen floor. Soot was crusted over every inch, so that he couldn't tell anything about it, but when he picked it up and tilted it he could feel something move inside it. He began to poke at the encrusted filth with a knife. It fell away in flakes like old paint. He kept going at one side and uncovered two sets of hinges. It was a box of some sort.

Callie came back in, damp and clean, and watched as he chipped away at the box.

"I wonder how long it's been up there?" Josh said.

"It looks pretty old. What do you think it's made of?"

"Metal, I think. Iron? I'm not sure."

At that moment, the lights went out. They sat suspended for a few seconds, waiting for them to flicker back on, but they didn't.

Callie got up. "I wonder if it's just us? I'll have a look." She went to the front door and looked out through the snow. There wasn't a light to be seen anywhere.

"Looks like a power cut," she said, coming back into the

kitchen. "I'd better get the smithy fire going in case it's off for a while. It'll take ages to warm up if the heating's off and it all cools down. You carry on. I'll only be a few minutes."

Josh went back to work on the box, though it was hard to see what he was doing with only the dim, pearly light from the snow-filled sky.

Callie came back from lighting the fire and began to look for candles, and Rose and George came back over from the garden, looking grim. Rose went straight through the kitchen, lost in thought.

"Power's out for miles around," said George. "The man in the fish van stopped to tell us. How will you get on at the cottage, Josh? It's all electric, isn't it?"

"Yes." He hadn't thought of that.

"Rose and I thought that maybe you and your mum would do better here. We've plenty of spare beds."

"Thanks. That's really kind. I'll ask her." He put down the knife. "I suppose I ought to go back and see what's happening."

"I'll take you round in the car," said George. "By the way, did the cat turn up yet?"

"She was stuck up the smithy chimney," said Callie, "sitting on this." She gestured at the box.

"Very interesting I'm sure. We'll have a look later, but I ought to take Josh home now."

"Thanks. I'll get my jacket."

The snow didn't look so heavy when they were in the car, driving through it. In a few minutes they were back at the cottage.

"I'll come in and see if your mother wants to come down to us."

Josh opened the door and found himself facing a suitcase. In the kitchen Anna was packing food away in boxes. She turned when she heard them.

"Oh Josh, I'm glad you're back. Go and pack your stuff up, would you?"

"Are we going to stay with the Fergusons?"

She looked blank. "No. We're going home. David and Susan phoned. Their washing machine's flooded our flat again. Susan's been in for a look and some of the kitchen ceiling's come down." She seemed to notice George for the first time. "Thanks for bringing Josh back. The power's gone off."

"I know. We wondered if you wanted to stay with us until it's back on. We've still got heat and cooking and so on."

She looked flustered. "Thank you. That's very kind, but we need to go home."

"But mum, we can't!"

"Why not? I'm sorry, Josh, but ..."

"Because ... it's our holiday ... and you haven't finished your book ... and ..." His voice trailed away. He couldn't say *Because I promised the Winter King I would come back.* "Surely David and Susan can sort things out? It's their fault, after all."

"Well, I'll let you get on," said George, sensing a brewing argument. "Goodbye, Josh. I hope you'll come back and see us soon, when things are better."

"Yes," said Josh miserably. He had never felt so frustrated, so powerless, in his entire life.

⁂

Half an hour later they were packed up, the car was loaded and the cottage keys had been handed back. All the time Josh had been trying to persuade Anna to go to the Fergusons' instead of going home, but she was adamant.

They drove slowly down the track away from the cottage.

"At least stop and let me go in and say goodbye."

"All right. Just five minutes though. I'm sure it's getting heavier."

He climbed from the car and trudged heavily up the path. Callie's face when she opened the door told him that she already knew.

"I'm sorry," he said miserably. "She won't listen. There's nothing I can do. I'll get back as soon as I can, somehow."

"Does it matter anyway?" she asked. "He said there was nothing anyone could do."

"But he called me, and he said he needs me close to keep him here. And I promised to come back."

She lifted her head and looked him in the eye for the first time. "Then come back. Quickly."

8. On the Road

They didn't talk. Anna was concentrating on driving in the snow, and Josh Wasn't Talking To Her – not that she seemed to have noticed.

By now they should have been able to see the St Andrews skyline, the Cathedral and St Rule's Tower poking out of the mass of roofs, but there was nothing to be seen but a featureless grey-white swirl of air as they came slowly down the long hill.

There wasn't much traffic on the road, although there was only a couple of inches of snow lying. No one would have thought anything about it, if it had been winter.

"Can we stop and get some lunch?"

His mother frowned. "I think we should get down the road as soon as possible."

"Oh, come on, mum; I'm starving – and it'll be ages before we get home."

"Well, all right – if we can find anywhere that hasn't shut because of the power cut. Just half an hour though."

They crept along South Street until they found a parking space.

"That looks open." Josh pointed at the window of the West Port Café, through which he could see candles flickering.

Heads down against the snow, they crossed the road and pushed the door open.

Although there were candles on the tables there were no customers inside. After a few seconds a waitress appeared from the kitchen.

"I'm sorry, we're shut. We can't cook."

"Oh no," groaned Josh, "I'm starving."

"I don't suppose you could just make us a sandwich, could you?" said Anna. "It's just that I don't know how long it'll take us to drive home in this."

"Well ..." The woman sighed. "How about some soup? We made it earlier and it's still hot."

"Thank you. That would be great."

They sat down and the waitress disappeared into the kitchen again. Outside the snow continued relentlessly. Josh thought of the Winter King in his cave and felt a sharp stab of sorrow and guilt and anger all mixed together, that he had let him down.

The waitress reappeared with two bowls of lentil soup and a plate of crusty bread and butter. They ate in silence. Josh knew his mother would be worried about the drive: she wasn't very keen on driving at the best of times.

The soup was good: thick and tasty and – yes – still pretty hot. Josh ate it as slowly as possible, trying to think of something that might delay them further, but no idea would come.

"This is on the house," said the waitress, putting two slices of chocolate cake that they hadn't asked for down in front of them.

"Great! Thanks," said Josh.

Anna looked at her watch. "I think we should go."

"Oh come on, mum. We can't leave this, it would be rude. Anyway, it's too good to leave." He shoved another forkful into his mouth.

All too soon however, he had finished the last mouthful and his mother was paying for the soup. As they left, the waitress was blowing out the candles and preparing to close up.

They cleared the car windows and the lights before they got back in. The snow was definitely lying more thickly now, three or four inches of it.

"It's all right," Anna said, half to herself. "It's a major route. They'll have the snow ploughs out clearing it."

They set off again.

❊❊❊

George looked at the box and gave it an experimental prod with the end of the screwdriver. "I reckon it's made of iron. I think it must be some sort of strongbox, and the Smith put it in that recess up the chimney for safe keeping. I wonder how long it's been there?"

He tilted it gently, listened to something slide from end to end. "I hope that's gold coins I hear in there. Let's have another go at getting it open."

At that moment Rose passed through the kitchen. "George," she said without looking round as she passed. "I think we should bring in as much wood as we can, and coal. We'll need to keep the fire going."

"All right dear." He put the screwdriver down. "I'll have a try a bit later. I'd better do the wood now."

When he'd gone Callie looked disconsolately round the empty kitchen. She didn't usually mind being on her own, but just at that moment she felt terribly lonely. She picked up the box and the screwdriver and took them up to her room, where the kitten was curled on the bed, and at least she could listen to her radio, since it ran on batteries.

She soon gave up on the radio though. No matter what station she tried to tune in to, all she could get were crackles and whines. With a sigh, she turned back to the box and began to work at the edge opposite the hinges.

"Mum, are you sure this is a good idea?" asked Josh as they edged out of St Andrews. The car heater was on full, but it didn't seem to be having much effect. There were two cars creeping along ahead of them, headlights on. Josh looked at his watch: two fifteen.

"It'll be fine once we reach the motorway," she replied absently, concentrating on the car in front.

There were flakes of soot all over the carpet, and her hands were filthy. Whey hadn't she thought to put a newspaper down? Rose would do her nut when she saw it. Oh well, no point in stopping now. She had just managed to wedge the tip of the screwdriver in between the lid of the box and the base. She twisted the handle of the screwdriver, trying to use it to lever the lid open. The first few times it just slipped out, but then she seemed to get some purchase and she felt the lid give, fractionally. She moved the screwdriver slightly further along and tried again. The lid moved a bit more. Everything else forgotten for the moment, she continued to prise the lid loose, until with a creak of protest and a shower of soot the hinges freed themselves and she lifted back the lid of the box.

Inside was a small, cloth-wrapped bundle and a sheaf of folded yellowed paper. She took out the little parcel and unwrapped it to reveal a small bottle. It looked as though it was glass, but it was so smeared and clouded by its time up the chimney that it was hard to tell. The neck was stoppered tightly. She made to open the bottle, then thought better of it, put it down, and picked up the papers instead.

They felt stiff and fragile as she unfolded them, to find that they were covered in spidery black writing. She got her torch and shone the light on the writing, trying to decipher it. At first she couldn't make it out at all, but as she concentrated, the letters seemed to untwist themselves and make sense. She began to read.

⁂

My name is Agnes Blair. I am sixteen years old and I am afraid.

⁂

They'd lost sight of the cars that had been in front of them. Anna was hunched over the wheel, staring into the flying snow. As soon as they'd gone through Guardbridge the weather had seemed to get much worse and they'd lost sight of the rest of their little convoy.

"Mum, we're never going to get to the motorway."

"Yes we will. We'll be all right once we get to Cupar." She seemed to think she could will the car through the snow.

There was no use arguing. He shut up again and hunched deeper into his jacket.

***

Oblivious to her surroundings, oblivious to the cold, Callie read what Agnes had left behind so many years ago, word by laborious word, for it was still difficult to decipher the writing. She drew a sharp breath, picked up the bottle again and stared at it as though it too was a message from the past.

"That's it!" she said to herself. "That's it!" She got to her feet, staring at the snow-filled sky. "Josh, come back! I know the answer!"

***

They were nearly at the big roundabout before Dairsie when, without warning, a wall of snow hit them, so thick that for a few seconds they were completely blinded. The car slewed across the road as Anna tried to get her bearings, and then the snow suddenly diminished again and they could see.

Josh gasped. "Mum – look out!"

There was a tractor heading straight for them. He heard his mother scream as she yanked the wheel hard to the left and then the car skidded off the road and into the snow-filled ditch that ran alongside and stopped abruptly.

9. Off the Road

Callie stood by the window to make the most of what little light there was and shone the torch on the papers as she read Agnes' story again. From time to time she glanced down at the little glass bottle on her bed. Finally she folded the papers again and put them back in the box.

"That's it, cat," she said to Chutney Mary. "Agnes took the bottle from the Queen of Summer and they must have been meant to take it back, but they never did. That's why she's dying – it belongs in her kingdom. We can do something. The King's bound to know how we can take it back. I need to get to the cave." She looked out of the window again. "Oh, Josh, why did you have to go just then?"

Suddenly she gave a squeak of exasperation with herself. "Idiot! You've got his phone number."

She scrambled in her desk for her phone and found Josh's number. It rang and rang and rang, but there was no reply. She sent him a text, pushed the box and its contents under her bed hoping her grandparents would have forgotten about it, and took the phone downstairs with her.

George and Rose were in the kitchen listening to the wind-up radio. The freak weather seemed to be affecting the whole country; in fact it wasn't as bad here as in many other places. There were numerous power cuts, but the electricity companies were hopeful that power would be restored everywhere in the next twenty-four hours.

There were candles in jam jars all over the house now, ready to be lit, and a big fire burning in the smithy hearth. There wasn't much else they could do. Surprisingly, it was the usually unflappable Rose who seemed most upset by events, constantly on the move, looking out the window, unable to sit still.

"Shall I make some tea?" asked George.

"Yes please dear. That would be nice."

There was a knock at the door.

***

The driver brought the tractor to a halt as quickly as he could in the road conditions, jumped down and ran back to where the car had ploughed off the road and into the ditch, his heart in his mouth at what he might find.

The car sat at an angle, nose down and tilted over to one side. As he reached it the driver's door opened and a dazed looking woman got out.

"Are you all right?" he yelled.

"Yes, I think so." She reached into the car. "Can you manage, Josh?"

"Yeah." A teenage boy clambered out of the car, shaking his head to clear it. "I'm fine. It's okay." He shook off the woman's proffered hand.

"I didn't see you until it was too late," the woman said.

"That great blast of snow just came out of nowhere and ..."

"At least you're both all right. Where were you trying to get to?"

"The motorway, to get back to Edinburgh."

"You wouldn't have got through anyway. The road's shut just the other side of Dairsie – there's big snowdrifts. I doubt they'll clear them today. Is there somewhere local you can stay?"

Josh saw his mother's shoulders slump in defeat. "Yes, if we could just get the car back on the road."

"That's easy. I can pull you out of the ditch. Get in the cab to keep warm and I'll hook her up."

They climbed up into the high cab of the tractor, squashed together beside the driver. He reversed back to the car and jumped down again with a rope which he attached to the tow point of the car and the front of the tractor.

"Let's see now," he said, climbing back up. He put the tractor in reverse and they watched as the rope grew taut. For a second, nothing else happened, then the car began to move, and in a moment it was free of the ditch.

They all climbed down again to check the car for any obvious signs of damage, but apart from a broken indicator, it looked fine.

"See if she'll start," suggested their rescuer. Incredibly, the car started first time, as he removed the tow rope and coiled it up.

"I'm going through St Andrews to Brownhills farm. You can follow me if you're going that way – might make it easier."

"Oh thank you, yes, we will." Anna was close to tears. Shock, Josh supposed. His own head ached dully, and so did his left shoulder, where he'd been thrown against the seat belt. His feet were so cold he could hardly feel them.

He climbed back into the passenger seat and they set off behind the reassuringly solid bulk of the tractor. It seemed to shelter them from the worst of the snow, and the going seemed a bit easier in this direction. Probably just because they didn't have so far to go, thought Josh, and there was a reasonable chance of them getting there.

Forty minutes later, they were waving goodbye to their good samaritan as he turned off into Brownhills farmyard.

"Not far now," Anna said, "and it's not nearly so bad here."

It was true; although the snow was thicker than when they had set out, there was less of it lying than there had been even as close by as St Andrews.

"I hope the Fergusons really meant it when they said we were welcome to stay. If not, we'll just have to get the keys to the cottage back."

***

"I'll get it," said Callie and went to open the front door. She gaped with astonishment when she found Josh and Anna standing outside.

"Josh ... thank goodness. You came back."

"We had to," said Anna, as Rose and George appeared in the hallway. "The road was blocked, and anyway, we came off the road and ended up in a snowdrift."

"Oh." Callie had thought somehow he'd come back because of her message.

"Let them in, Callie, for goodness sake. They look half-frozen." Rose shoved her aside and pulled the door wide.

"We were hoping your offer of a bed was still open."

"Of course it is. Come away in and let's get you warmed up. The car came off the road you say? Are the two of you sure you're not hurt?" Rose was in full flow now, shepherding them towards the kitchen.

"Yes; there was this awful flurry of snow and then a tractor ..."

Callie caught Josh's arm and pulled him back. "Did you get my text?"

"No. My phone's in the car boot."

"I found something – in the box from the chimney. I think I've found what was taken from the Queen of Summer."

He looked completely bewildered. "I don't understand. Can I get warm first? I'm frozen."

"Sorry. Of course." She gave up for the moment, although she was seething with impatience.

In the kitchen, Rose was making hot chocolate. "This'll help. George is running the bath and then you can get into some dry clothes."

"You still have hot water?"

"Yes. There's a back boiler in the smithy."

"What's that?" asked Josh.

"It's a boiler behind the fire. The fire heats the water," said Callie.

"And we've got gas for cooking," Rose went on, "so you'll be as well here as anywhere just now."

An hour later they were all in the smithy, warm, dry and, for the time being, safe. Anna had phoned their neighbours to ask them to do what they could in the meantime and seemed resigned to being stuck in Pitmillie for the moment. Josh's head still ached. He wanted nothing more than to lie down and go to sleep. His mother and Rose and George were chatting away inexhaustibly. On the other side of the fire he could see Callie fretting.

Eventually she could stand it no longer. "I'll go and make the spare beds up, Rose. Come on, Josh, you can give me a hand."

"Thank you, Callie, but leave Josh where he is. He looks worn out."

"No, I'm fine. I need to get up or I'll fall asleep."

Callie led him to her room and pulled the box out from under the bed. She let Josh open it while she lit three candles in jars and found her torch again. She glanced out of the window as she did so.

"It's stopped snowing."

"Well, that's something." Josh examined the bottle, rubbing at the cloudy glass with one finger, trying to see if there was anything inside.

"Go on – read the letter-diary thing. I'll go and make the beds up."

She came back ten minutes later to find Josh reading the last page, a frown on his face.

"What happened to her?"

"I don't know. That's all there was."

They were silent for a few seconds, considering the fates that might have befallen Agnes.

"But she was only sixteen," said Josh. "They wouldn't have ..."

"Yes they would," said Callie fiercely. "Age made no difference. If they thought she was a witch they most likely killed her."

"She *was* a witch."

"Or thought she was. She doesn't seem to have done anything. Anyway, that's not the point. She and the others brought this bottle out of the Kingdom of Summer to change the weather. The King said some of the Queen's power had been stolen and that's why all this," she waved vaguely towards the window, "is happening."

"But they didn't steal this; she gave it to them."

"If Agnes is telling the truth. But maybe they stole it. Agnes wouldn't want to say that on top of everything else. It would be easier to pretend they'd been given it."

From downstairs, Rose called "Tea's ready."

"We need to get back to the cave and show the bottle to the Winter King, and if this *is* what's been stolen, we have to find a way to return it," said Josh.

"Exactly."

"But how are we going to get back to him? We can hardly suggest popping out for a nice walk in this."

Callie looked triumphant. "We'll wait until everyone's asleep, then we'll drive there."

Josh burst out laughing. "If only!"

"No, I'm serious. Listen: my parents' car is in their garage. I've given you the downstairs spare room, so all we have to do is wait until everyone's asleep then go and get it. I've got the house keys and I know where the car keys are."

Josh seriously considered shaking her. Instead, with an effort, he kept his voice level. "Neither of us can drive."

"*I* can. George taught me on the road at the old airfield on the way to Fife Ness. Rose doesn't know – she'd be furious with him – but I can drive."

"But you're not old enough!"

She shrugged. "All right. Let's hear *your* idea."

"I don't have one."

"Well, then?"

"Remember, I've been in a car today and look what happened."

"But you said yourself, it's not nearly so bad here. And it's stopped snowing."

As if in support, they heard the sound of a car outside just then and watched from the window as it went slowly up the road, its headlights on although it was barely six in the evening and the middle of summer.

"You're mad."

"Is that the best you can do? I get that at school all the time. Come on Josh, *think*. Really think."

He looked again at Agnes' spidery writing and at the little bottle.

"Okay, okay. But please let me get some sleep first. I can't think properly any more."

"Callie! Josh! Come on." It was Rose again.

"Just coming," Callie called back. She reached a hand out to Josh and half-pulled him to his feet. "Have you tea, then go to bed. I'll wake you when it's time."

He nodded, too tired to argue with her.

⁂

Eleven o'clock.

Josh and Anna had long since gone to bed, exhausted by the day's events. Callie had followed soon after. George was making up the smithy fire so it would burn slowly all night. Luath at her side, Rose walked the boundaries of her snowy garden, muttering quietly to herself.

She had started at the gate, and was walking slowly all the way round, keeping as close as she could to the garden wall. Luath was silent but uneasy, ears pricked, and she kept one hand on his neck as she walked.

When she arrived back at the gate she sent him away to the door of the house. From her pocket she produced three candles, squat little night lights that wouldn't fall or blow over. She set them down on the path in front of the gate. Straightening, she took a deep breath and held her hands, palm-down, over the candles. Tiny flames caught on the wicks, blue at first, then green and as the flames grew, finally golden.

When the flames had grown as tall as she was she caught them in her hands and braided them together. She lowered her hands and from the braided flames a net of light began to form, spreading out along the walls and arching up and over the house and garden until the whole thing was surrounded by a web of silver-white filaments that glowed for a few seconds and then disappeared, and all that was left was the old woman watching three tiny candle flames waver in the cold air.

She turned wearily back towards the house where Luath still waited. "Sleep easy tonight dog. Nothing from the Frozen Lands will enter this place for this night at least."

They went in and she locked the front door behind her.

"Josh! Josh!" Callie shook Josh's shoulder as she hissed in his ear. "Come on, wake up. It's time to go."

He stirred, then opened his eyes. She saw, in the torchlight, his expression change as he remembered what was happening.

"Oh, no," he groaned.

10. Betsy

They crept out through the back door, so that their footsteps in the snow wouldn't be so easily seen the next morning, and climbed over the garden wall out into the lane that ran down the side of the house.

Remembering how cold he'd been in the car earlier that day, Josh had piled layers of clothes on, only to find, now that he was outside, that it wasn't as cold as he had expected.

Callie was muffled in an old navy duffel coat that was too big for her and that Josh hadn't seen before. *Does she have any new clothes?* Josh found himself wondering irrelevently. She carried a small rucsac containing Agnes' box, a flask of coffee, a bar of chocolate and, as an afterthought, half a bottle of whisky.

It was a quarter to one in the morning, and apart from them, no one was out on the darkened streets. The power still hadn't come back on and it was fortunate that the moon was still full and the sky – for the moment – was clear. They had torches as well, but it seemed best to save the batteries: they didn't want to find themselves without light in the middle of Fife Ness at night.

They reached Callie's house without incident. It was down the road that led to the beach and they should have been able to hear the rhythmic scour and suck of the waves, but it was strangely muted tonight.

Callie unlocked the door and they went in. It was cold as only an empty house can be and Josh found it hard to imagine it as it must usually have been before Callie's parents left for Ghana.

"Wait here. I'll get the keys." She disappeared upstairs, leaving him in the sitting room.

He walked around the room, peering at things, thinking of them as clues to Callie's parents. He must ask her tomorrow to let him see a photograph.

He made his way idly to the window that faced along the road towards the beach and looked at the faint, moonlit shapes of the road and trees and the other houses nearby.

What was taking Callie so long? Presumably the keys weren't where she thought they were, after all.

He was about to turn away from the window and follow her upstairs to see what the problem was, when a flicker of movement caught his eye.

Something was moving up the road from the beach.

He watched, mesmerized, as whatever it was drew close enough to see properly by moonlight. Not *it* at all, but *them.* There were three figures moving up the road towards the house and the village, human shaped but not, somehow, like people. Unconsciously, he drew back from the window.

At that moment, Callie came back into the room, waving her lit torch.

"Got them."

"Turn that off!"

"What?"

"Turn the torch off – quickly."

She fumbled with the switch and it was suddenly dark again. "What is it?"

"Look."

Moonlight gleamed off the approaching figures. They moved slowly, stooped as though into a powerful wind, although it was calm.

Callie pulled at Josh's jacket. "Upstairs – we can watch from there without being seen."

They hurried upstairs and she led him into a small bedroom whose window also faced the beach.

The figures were closer now and clearer. They were taller than men, with thick, powerful limbs. Their faces were broad and flat, with a nose and mouth, but no visible eyes or ears, and they swung their heads to left and right as they came steadily closer to the house.

"What are they?" breathed Callie.

"I don't know. They look as if they're made of glass ... or ..."

"... or ice." She finished the sentence for him.

"They must be the Winterbringers the King talked about."

"What are they doing? Where are they going?"

He shook his head. "We'll have to ask the King." The Winterbringers were only about thirty metres from the house now. "At least they can't see or hear."

"I'm not so sure about that."

They watched the creatures' heads swing from side to side as they walked.

When they were almost level with the house, they

stopped without warning and stood very still, for all the world as though they were listening.

Callie and Josh stood frozen, not at all convinced now that the creatures were as blind and deaf as they looked.

The creatures lifted their blank faces and sniffed. Callie and Josh could hear the sound of the air being sucked into their icy nostrils. Then, as one, they turned their massive heads towards the house.

Callie gave a little gasp. "They know we're here," she whispered, terrified.

For what felt like a long time, no one moved, but then the creatures seemed to come to life again. They moved out of Josh and Callie's line of vision and after a few seconds she pulled him through to another room, this time with a window overlooking the road.

The ice-things were directly below them, right outside the front door, pressing and pushing against it. Josh could hear the scrape of their icy hands on the wood. Speechless with fear, he heard Callie whimper beside him.

Suddenly, the Winterbringers stopped moving again, frozen and motionless against the door and then, without warning or explanation, they stepped away from it back onto the road and continued on their lumbering way.

Josh found he was on his knees, though he couldn't remember kneeling down. He could hear Callie's sobbing in the darkness beside him. His own hands were shaking and he knew that if he tried to stand up at the moment he'd fall over.

He reached for Callie, found her hand and the two of them clung to each other until the worst of the terror receded.

"Where do you think they're going?"

"I don't know. I don't care, so long as it's away from here. Come on, let's get the car."

There was a door from the kitchen out to the garage. They had to put the torches on now, because there were no windows. Josh gaped when he saw the car. It looked ancient.

"What sort of car is *that?"* It had wood round the windows, as though it was a house on wheels.

"A Morris Traveller."

"Are you sure it works?"

"Yes – and it's *she,* not *it* – she's my dad's pride and joy. Her name's Betsy."

"You dad has a car with a *name?"*

Even in the semi-dark, he could see her smiling.

"He's had her since he was a medical student. She's one of the family, really. He's got enough spare parts to build about another three, I think – just in case anything goes wrong, but it hardly ever does."

"Betsy ... okay."

Callie unlocked the doors and they got in. The seats were faded red leather, lovingly polished. The interior of the car smelled of something Josh couldn't quite identify.

Callie heard him sniffing. "Beeswax," she said, "to keep the leather and the wood happy. Well, here goes." She turned the ignition key, and somewhat to Josh's surprise, the engine started first time.

Leaving the engine running, they got out to open the garage door. Before they went back in they crept cautiously round the corner of the house to look up and down the road, but there was no sign of the

Winterbringers except patches of sand and weed and shells mixed with the churned snow. The door itself was marked and scraped as though by heavy nails.

Callie stared at them, a horrible realization dawning in her mind. "Josh? That's what was outside our front door a couple of mornings ago."

He looked more carefully, remembering the front door of The Smithy. "You're right. Do you think that's what disturbed you during the night?"

"I don't know. I didn't see them clearly. But what if that's where they're heading now?"

"Rose and George and my mum ..."

"We have to warn them!"

They hurried back to the car. Callie switched the headlights on, then changed her mind and put them off again. "They'll see us coming a mile off with lights on. There's enough moonlight to see by."

She put the car into gear and they moved rather jerkily out of the garage and turned onto the road back to the village. They went slowly, peering ahead, not wanting to come suddenly on the ice creatures. Josh had to admit that she seemed to know what she was doing, although her gear changing was a bit jumpy.

Where the beach road reached the village she stopped and turned off the engine. They listened intently but there was no sound that suggested the Winterbringers were near.

There were tracks in the snow though: of big mis-shapen feet mixed with clots of sand and fragments of shell and weed. They went in the direction of The Smithy.

They looked at each other and nodded in agreement,

got out of the car and set off, following the tracks, keeping close to the wall that bounded the church yard to make themselves less obvious.

Almost level with the church gate they stopped, staring up the road that led to the Smithy. Three bulky figures stood just outside the garden wall. The house itself was in darkness, but there was a tiny flicker of light from behind the garden gate.

The Winterbringers were swaying from side to side as though unsure of what to do. Every so often, one of them would put a hand out to the wall and push against it, but pull its hand back almost immediately, as though the wall had burnt it.

As they touched the wall Callie thought she saw a network of faint glowing lines in the air above the house and garden.

"Look," she whispered to Josh.

"What?"

"The lines."

But he didn't seem to understand what she meant.

The Winterbringers seemed to reach some sort of agreement and moved lumpishly towards the garden gate. This time all three put their arms out towards it at once and pushed against it with their hands, but as they did so the flickering lights behind the gate grew taller and stronger and the network of filaments appeared in the air again.

The ice creatures made a sound that might have been a cry of pain and moved away from the gate and the lines of light disappeared as the flames behind the gate sank once more.

The creatures turned and began to move towards where Josh and Callie stood watching.

"Run!"

They took to their heels as the figures advanced along the road towards them. Although Josh knew perfectly well that they were going much too slowly to catch him and Callie, it didn't stem the panic he could feel bubbling up inside him.

They reached Betsy. Callie fumbled the keys and dropped them as she made to open the door.

"Come on, come on!" Josh fidgeted anxiously, looking back to the road junction behind them, where the Winterbringers would surely appear at any moment.

"I'm trying. There – get in."

She started the motor and tried to move off, but the wheels just spun uselessly in the snow. She tried again, but the same thing happened.

"Try second gear," he yelled at her. "My mum did that in St Andrews."

"You'll have to get out and push us off."

"What?!"

"Hurry up. Look – here they come." The first of the Winterbringers had just appeared around the corner, only a hundred metres away.

Josh forced himself to get out of the car, stumbled round to the rear and yelled, "Okay – go!"

Callie put the car into second gear and let the clutch out. The wheels spun; Josh pushed against the rear window with all his strength and fell headfirst into the snow as the car lurched out of the hollow it had been stuck in.

He heard Callie yelling at him, picked himself up, half ran, half crawled to the car, and threw himself in.

Callie accelerated away and this time the car jerked forwards straight away. She yanked the wheel too hard and they skidded round the corner and then they were away, Josh watching the receding figures of the ice creatures through the back window.

For a few moments, neither of them spoke. Josh brushed the snow off his clothes as best he could and put on his seatbelt, while Callie concentrated on the unfamiliar demands of driving on snow.

"That was a bit too exciting," Josh said finally.

"You can say that again. I wonder what would have happened if they had caught us?"

"I'd rather not think about that," he said with a shudder. "What do you think they were trying to do at Rose and George's house?"

"Get in, of course."

"Yes, I know, but why? When they were trying the door of your parents' house I thought that must be because they knew that we were in there somehow, and that we were ... connected ... to what's going on. But in that case, why your grandparents' house now, when neither of us is there?"

They had reached Crail. Callie was silent, trying to think of an answer, as they eased their way through the village and turned off for Fife Ness. There was definitely less snow down here.

"I don't know. I hadn't thought about it until you said it, but they went past lots of other houses without trying to get in, didn't they?

"Here's another thing though. Why couldn't they get into the garden? They've done it before. When they were pushing against the gate there were lots of lines of light around the house – in the air. What were they?"

Josh turned to look at her. "Callie, I never saw that, and I was watching, just like you."

"I don't understand. They were definitely there."

"Callie, I'm sorry, but I didn't see anything. Maybe you were dazzled by something, or ... stress made you see whatever it was."

She gave him a freezing look and they drove in silence for a few minutes.

She had the headlights on full beam now, as they came down the road towards the golf course. "This is the closest we can leave the car." She stopped and turned off the engine. For a moment she left the headlights on, illuminating a landscape smoothed by snow and deathly quiet.

"Better not run the battery down." She switched off the lights. They made no move to get out, letting their eyes grow accustomed to the dark, unwilling to leave the relative security of the car.

"Well, we've got this far. I suppose we'd better go the rest of the way," said Callie.

"Come on then," said Josh, opening the door reluctantly.

11. The Bottle

The moon was still clear of cloud, though they could see it stacking up to the North and East. They walked side by side, as close as they could, torches trained on the uneven ground just ahead of them.

They didn't talk: they didn't dare. An immense oppressive silence had settled over the night, against which even the snow-muffled sound of their footsteps sounded shockingly loud.

The quietness troubled Josh. There was something unsettling, *dangerous* about it. They reached the path along the shore and he realized why.

There was no sound of waves. The sea had frozen. The moon glinted off moving water thirty metres or so offshore, but closer in it was a ruffled sheet of ice.

They had come to a halt, staring incredulously at the sight before them.

"I've seen this on one of George's old home movies. It was ages ago – back in nineteen sixty something; the hardest winter anyone can remember. It's never happened here since."

It was obvious now: it was the absence of wave sounds that was so eerie. The sea was never silent.

Not in normal times.

Josh roused himself. "Come on."

They walked parallel to the silent shore for five minutes, slowing down as they rounded the final corner and saw ahead of them the rocky outcrop that housed Constantine's Cave.

After the relative brightness of the moonlight on the snow, it took their eyes a little time to adjust to the darker surroundings of the cave, even with the torches on. When they did so, Callie gasped. "Oh no!"

The Winter King lay sprawled against the back wall of the cave, one hand outstretched as though towards something just out of reach.

"Is he dead?" she asked, dreading the answer, as Josh knelt beside him.

Josh touched his face, felt for a pulse in his neck. His skin was so cold that its touch almost burned him.

"No. He's got a pulse."

Callie came and knelt beside him and gently shook his shoulder. "Wake up! Please wake up. We think we've found something – we think we can save her."

At first there was no response, but then his blue-veined eyelids flickered and opened and he held her mute in his wintry gaze.

She tugged the rucsac off her shoulders and reached into it for the whisky bottle.

"Help him sit up."

Josh and Callie tugged him into a sitting position against the cave wall, the frost-rimmed carvings stark in the torchlight. He still hadn't spoken.

"Here," said Callie, taking the top off the bottle. "Drink some of this."

Obediently, he took the bottle and swallowed and

gasped and swallowed again, and handed the bottle back.

"Can you hear me?" Josh asked.

He nodded.

"We found something. We think we can help you save her – the Queen of Summer."

He caught Josh's wrist in a grip like a fetter of ice. "Show me."

"Oww! All right, all right. That's why we've come. Let go."

Callie pulled the narrow black box out of the rucsac and set it on the ground beside the King. "We found this stuck inside the chimney in my grandparents' house. It's been there for more than three hundred years. It all makes sense."

She opened the box, unwrapped the little bottle and held it out to him. He took it and turned it between his fingers, frowning.

"But what is this?"

"See for yourself." She handed him the bundle of papers. "She wrote it all down."

He handed the bottle back to her, took the papers and unfolded them. He stared at them, one after another, turning them this way and that, then looked up at her.

"What are these?"

"Read them – it's the story of how the bottle was taken from the Queen of Summer."

"I do not understand what you mean – read? But this bottle ..." He shook his head sadly. "This cannot save her."

"Can't you read?" asked Josh.

"I do not understand the word."

"Okay. But please, listen. I'm sure the bottle has something to do with what's been happening. Go on Callie."

Callie put the bottle back in the box, took the papers from the King and shuffled them into order. She glanced at Josh, then began to read.

She didn't look up until she reached the end, and when she did so it was to find the King staring at her in wonder.

"These marks say that?"

She nodded.

"Then where is it?"

"The bottle?" Josh said, puzzled. "We showed you. It's here." He held it up again.

"No. Not the bottle. I told you it could not be that. Agnes Blair took some of the Queen's power from her kingdom, but it was not this bottle. It was the feather. The Kingfisher feather. It was part of her."

Josh and Callie gaped at him.

"But ..." Callie opened the box and looked again, though she knew there was nothing else in it. "There was no feather. Just the story and the bottle. I'm sorry."

She felt crushed by failure. How must the King feel? To understand at last what had happened and still be helpless to put it right.

The look on his face was almost unbearable.

Josh watched the other two, abject with disappointment, but at the back of his mind, something nagged at him. He waited for it to surface, knowing from experience that if he tried to concentrate on it, it would slip further away.

Callie began to pack things away in the rucsac automatically, the beam of her torch catching a glinting icicle that hung from the cave roof.

Of course. That was it. Ice.

"The Winterbringers – the ice creatures."

"They are abroad?"

"They tried to get into my parents' house – and my grandparents' – when we were coming here," said Callie.

Together they explained what had happened.

"It sounds as though they acted with purpose," the King said, but he didn't sound interested.

"And what about the lines of light around the house? Did they make them?"

"No. They were to keep them out. They came from inside the house."

"That's it!" Josh nearly yelled. "The feather must be somewhere in the house – and they were trying to get it."

"You credit them with intelligence they do not have."

"But *something* made that net of light and kept them out," said Callie excitedly. "What else could it be?"

"Come on. You have to come back with us. We'll explain somehow, and find the feather and put things right."

"I cannot leave here. I grow weak. I will not be able to fight the forces of Winter if I leave here."

"Well, they're winning anyway," Josh retorted. "At least this way there's a chance." Even as he said it, he wondered to himself how long a feather could survive, but anything seemed better than to accept defeat in this cold cave. "You've got nothing left to lose."

The King looked at them both. "After what you have done, you deserve at least that I do not give up hope." He stretched out a hand and Josh took it, burning cold, and helped him to his feet. As he did so, he lost his own footing on the frost-slippery rocks and flung out his free hand in an effort to regain his balance.

The bottle flew from his grip. He watched in horror as it spun across the cave and smashed against the opposite wall.

There was a fugitive scent of honey and roses and summer rain, then it was lost in the cold sea air.

They stood in silence for a few seconds, then Callie walked slowly over and crouched down to look at the glittering shards more closely.

"Come here." Her voice sounded oddly strained.

They walked across the cave and looked down. The glass had shattered into jewel-coloured fragments, and among them lay a single feather, the perfect blue of a midsummer sky.

They stood, struck speechless, afraid to move in case the miraculous feather was to crumble to dust before their eyes.

Fittingly, it was the King who reached out at last and with tender care, picked it up.

It didn't crumble.

He raised it to his lips and kissed it gently, and looked and looked at it as though he could see the Queen of Summer before him.

"Come," he said, new strength in his voice, "you must take me to the place where Agnes Blair found her way into the Kingdom of Summer. Perhaps there is a chance to save Her and put all of this to rights, but we cannot have much time left."

He reached into his tunic and pulled out a pouch of deerskin that hung around his neck on a leather thong. Into this he gently put the feather, then tucked it safely back inside his clothes.

They left the cave behind and began to retrace their steps to the car. The King paused for a moment to look out over the ruffled ice that fringed the sea. He nodded sadly. "You are right. They are winning. Another few days and they will have won completely."

"Not if we can get the feather back to the Queen."

"No, perhaps not."

Away from the cave, it was apparent just how weak the King was. He walked slowly, leaning on Josh.

"Not far," said Callie encouragingly. "Look – you can see the car now."

The car was obviously something of deep strangeness to the King, but he had no time – or energy – to do anything but get into the back seat obediently. Callie took one last look back at the shore and started the engine.

The journey back was tense but uneventful. Callie managed to control the car far better than she had earlier and Josh found his hands gradually unclenching.

As they approached the village, Callie slowed down, alert for Winterbringers or tracks that would show where they had gone. There was no sight of the ice men, but sets of tracks led off across one of the fields roughly in the direction of East Neuk Cottages.

They got the car back into the garage without incident and closed and locked the door. The Winter King uncurled himself stiffly from the back seat and watched as Callie unlocked the door through to the house.

"What is this?" he asked.

She looked back at him. "It's a house. I don't suppose you have houses in the Frozen Lands." He shook his head. "I usually live here with my parents. They're not here just now, so I'm staying at my grandparents' house. So are Josh and his mum; they tried to leave earlier today – no, wait, it's yesterday by now – but the snow had blocked the road.

"I can't take you there – they'll think we're all mad. You can stay here just now; it must be better than the cave, anyway."

He nodded. "For now. As soon as morning comes you must find the stream that Agnes followed and make a boat like hers. Then we shall see if the Kingdom will let us in or if it is sealed."

"Sealed? I thought you said you could go to her?"

The King looked at the floor. "I hoped to. In truth, I do not know if it will be possible."

There didn't seem to be a lot to say to that.

"We should go now," said Josh. "Will you be all right?"

He nodded. "Go. Before they discover you are not in the house."

They checked the road from the windows before they went out and started cautiously up the road that led to the centre of the village.

"Do you think he'll be all right?"

"More all right than we will be if anything goes wrong. And definitely more all right than we'll be if Rose finds we've been out."

It was almost four in the morning and beginning to grown light. They made their way wearily back towards The Smithy, hugging the churchyard wall to make themselves less conspicuous.

As they turned the corner into Smithy Road they both stopped. Away across the fields they could see not one, but two groups of Winterbringers: the three they had seen earlier – or at least they assumed so – and another pair. They were heading back into the village but so far they didn't seem to have noticed Josh and Callie.

Glancing towards The Smithy Callie saw again the net of light in the sky around it. "Look," she whispered to Josh, pointing, but he was more concerned with the Winterbringers.

"Come on," he said, pulling Callie towards the lane at the side of The Smithy. The house (thank goodness) was still in darkness, but just inside the garden gate three candles burned with tall golden flames. Callie stopped and stared at them intently.

"Do you think these could be something to do with the lights in the sky?"

"*What* lights? I keep telling you I can't see anything."

"*Look,* for goodness sake. They're there right now, just over the house."

Dutifully he looked. "Callie, I'm not sure what you think you can see, but there's nothing there. No lights. Nothing."

They glared at each other for a few seconds, until Callie said, "This is a stupid place to argue. Let's get inside."

"Okay."

They climbed back over the garden wall and let themselves in the back door.

"We'd better get back to our own rooms while the going's good I suppose," she said.

Josh nodded, so tired at the thought of his bed that he couldn't even summon the energy to speak.

"I'll see you at breakfast then." She turned to go, but he caught her sleeve.

"You're a great driver, you know."

"I know." She grinned, and headed for the stairs and bed.

As she opened her bedroom door carefully she could hear George's snores and Rose's heavy breathing, and Chutney Mary came purring from the bed to meet her.

Before she even took her coat off she went to the window and opened the curtains just enough to see out. Both groups of Winterbringers were in the field over the road from The Smithy, moving towards the sea. This time they didn't even pause as they passed the house.

Callie watched them out of sight, then went to bed.

12. Boat Building

Rose was up just after six, although she had been awake for an hour before that. Taking Luath with her, she walked slowly around the edge of the garden, as she had done the night before, checking for any signs that the Winterbringers had broken through her defences.

There were no traces of sand or shell or weed anywhere in the garden, just a bit of the back wall where the snow had been knocked off and some confused footprints between there and the back door. She stared at them hard for a minute, then dismissed them as unimportant: just some of the village kids larking about no doubt; certainly not the work of the ice-creatures.

When she reached the gate she put out the candles with a wave of her hand and bent to pick them up. As she did so she noticed the sea-flotsam signs of the Winterbringers on the other side of the gate and, inspecting it more closely, she could see the gouge marks from heavy, flat nails tearing at the wood. She shivered in spite of herself, picked up the candles and went back into the house.

In the hall, she picked up the phone. Nothing; the lines must be down. Sighing, she put it down again. She listened for a moment to see if anyone else was up and around, but the house was silent, or at least as close to silent as an old house ever gets, so she went into the kitchen, filled the washing-up bowl with water, and set it down on the kitchen table.

She looked intently into it for a few seconds, closed her eyes and said something under her breath, then opened them again and waited.

After about five minutes, the surface of the water grew cloudy, as though someone had poured milk into it, and then a face appeared, looking up out of the water.

"Oh, it's you," said the face.

"Don't sound so surprised," said Rose. "There's only the four of us, so I can't be that much of a shock."

"It's a bit early, that's all. I was asleep." Bessie Dunlop yawned as though to emphasize the fact, then looked at Rose more closely. "You don't look as though you've slept much."

"Och, I've not done badly, considering. Bessie, I'd to cast the net round the house last night. The Winterbringers are on the move. Only at night so far, but more of them and for longer, every night."

"Did it work?"

"Of course it did! They'll have to get a lot stronger before they can break through that."

Bessie's face grew serious. "The thing is, my dear, that they will."

"What was it like in town last night?"

"Cold. Dark. I feel sorry for all these modern people who got rid of their coal fires and gas cookers. I was quite cosy myself, considering. Have you spoken with the others yet?"

"No. I didn't want to disturb them too early."

"Hmmmf. I see ... whereas it doesn't matter if you wake me up?"

"You know perfectly well what I mean Bessie. The others have got families with them in the house whereas you ..."

"I am a Little Old Lady Alone. I know."

"Well, hardly. I'm not sure I'd describe you as a Lady, for one thing, and ..."

"I think we'll just stop there, thank you."

"Anyway," said Rose. "I had a thought."

Bessie waited, silent.

"Maybe together, we could force a way into the Kingdom."

Bessie sighed. "And if we could, what then?"

"I don't know," Rose admitted, "but there's nothing else I can think of to even try, and I'm not ready to give in just yet."

"That's the spirit, girl! Go on, get the others out of bed and let's get thinking. Maybe something new will occur to one of us. After all, it's not as if we've already been wracking our brains about this for years.

"And while you're waking them up," she added "I can get some clothes on instead of sitting freezing in my nightdress, staring into a pot of water."

The image of Bessie's face faded, and Rose was once more looking into a washing up bowl full of nothing more than water.

She sighed and prepared to summon the others.

Josh was running as fast as he could. Below his feet the snow had crusted over with ice. His feet broke through at every step, into the cold, soft snow below. He had to reach the cottage before the Winterbringers caught him. Even with its caved-in roof it would be a refuge from them. He just had to reach it before they reached him.

As he thought this, the ice ahead of and around him began to fold and ripple and crack. He slowed, fascinated almost against his will by what was going on at his feet.

As he did so the ice shaped itself finally and a forest of hands pushed up from its crackling surface, feeling blindly, reaching for him.

He swerved wildly, trying to elude the cold grasping fingers, but it was no good. They had him. They had him ...

"Josh, wake up! Come on; it's after ten." The hands had him, shaking him ...

"Hmmmf ... let go!"

"Josh! Get up. We need to get to work."

He woke properly then. The hand grasping his shoulder was Callie's, not something that had erupted from the icy ground.

"Sorry," he said, sitting up. "I must have been dreaming. Did you say after ten?"

"Yes, and the power's back on."

"Well, that's good anyway. What about the snow?"

"No more since last night, but it's very cold."

"Have you had breakfast?"

"Ages ago. Everyone's up but you. Your mum's been telling us all how much you like your sleep." She grinned evilly.

"Oh no," he groaned, pulling the pillow down over his head. "Don't give me any details please. I'll be through in a minute. Then you can all laugh at me."

When he got up he found everyone in the kitchen – as usual – listening to local radio. It was giving information about where there were still power cuts and phone lines down, which seemed to be a lot of places. The police were telling people to stay off the roads: very few were passable and more snow was expected later.

"It looks as if you'll be here until tomorrow at least," said George.

"Yes, it does," sighed Josh's mum. "I'm sorry to impose like this. I suppose we could go back to the cottage now the power's back on. We did pay for the whole week."

"You'll do no such thing," said Rose. "It'll be freezing cold up there. You're much better here with us. Anyway, we're all company for each other."

"Well, if you're sure ..."

They turned their attention back to the radio, listening to reports of weather conditions from the rest of the country. All the major rivers – even the Thames – had frozen. Cities were virtually cut off and panic buying had emptied supermarket shelves across the country.

Rose sniffed disdainfully. "At least folk here have a bit more sense than that. Don't these people know what store cupboards are for?"

"Probably not," said Callie, "but they'd say 'doesn't she know what a microwave's for?' about you."

"Much good their microwaves will be doing them now," retorted Rose, unimpressed.

Josh and Callie escaped to her room as soon as they could and pored over Agnes Blair's journal to find out as much as possible about what they had to try to do.

***

They made a tiny boat of birch bark, that could sit in the palm of your hand. They painted an eye on the prow, so it would find its way, then we each pricked our thumbs with Janet's knife and let a drop of blood fall into the boat so that it would know us.

Beatrix had a long coil of white silk thread. She tied one end to the boat and the other to a trailing branch, so the boat would find its way home, then set it down on the water of the tiny stream that flowed through Pitmillie.

***

"Well, that sounds clear enough," said Callie.

"Birch bark?"

"There's a birch tree in the back garden." She looked at him narrowly. "You do know what a birch tree looks like, don't you?"

"Yes, of course. No."

"It doesn't matter. I do. Knife, yes. White silk thread ... there's bound to be some in Rose's embroidery box ... paint ..."

"What about the stream? Where is it? Is it still there?"

"The only stream that flows through Pitmillie now is the one we walked beside when we saw the deer."

She frowned. "But it doesn't really go anywhere. It just peters out into a sort of a drainage ditch in the fields up the road a bit."

"Well, we'll just have to hope it's the right one." Josh folded Agnes' papers carefully and put them back in the box. "Should we go and see the King just now, do you think?"

Callie shook her head. "I think we should get everything ready first. But he was so weak last night – I think we need to hurry."

"Let's go and get this bark then and try to make a boat."

It was breathtakingly cold outside: much colder than it had been during the night. They stood looking at the birch tree.

"How much do you think we need?"

"Agnes said the boat fitted in the palm of her hand." Josh held his own hand up, trying to estimate.

"Okay. Keep an eye on the house. I don't want George to find me doing this." She pulled a penknife from her pocket and scored the bark carefully in a rectangle about twice the size of her hand. "That should be enough, shouldn't it?"

Josh nodded.

Callie levered up a corner of the bark with the point of the knife and began to peel it carefully away from the trunk.

It came away much more easily than she had expected, and a couple of minutes later she was holding a ragged-edged sheet of birch bark.

"Right. Let's get back to your room and make this boat. Do you think we're allowed to use glue?"

"I don't think Agnes would have had glue, do you?"

"I suppose not. I'll think of something. At least making models is something I'm good at."

Back in Callie's room Josh set to work with pen, paper and scissors to make a pattern for the boat before he cut the birch bark, while Callie went off to look for the thread.

When she came back he was surrounded by scraps of paper and was frowning at a new sheet.

"You *do* know what you're doing, don't you?" said Callie anxiously.

"Yeah – don't panic. I just want to make sure I've got it exactly right before I cut the bark. Have you got a craft knife or something?"

However much Callie stared at the drawing Josh was looking at, she couldn't see how it was going to turn into a boat.

"It doesn't look like a boat," she said, "but then I'm never any good at those maths things where you have to imagine something three dimensional into a flat shape."

He couldn't help but laugh. "You mean nets? They're easy."

"Maybe for you," Callie sighed, "but not for me. They must have left that bit out of my brain."

"The knife?"

"Oh, yes. I'll find one."

By the time she came back Josh had satisfied himself that the shapes were right. He drew his plan onto the smooth inner surface of the bark and began to cut as Callie watched. When he had finished he scored some lines, made a number of slits and set to work bending and weaving sections of bark into each other.

Ten minutes later it was done. In the palm of his hand Josh held a tiny boat of birch bark, shaped rather like a canoe, with a high prow and stern and a flat bottom. They looked at it proudly, as though it was their child.

"Wow. That's fantastic."

"Mmmn. I'm quite pleased with it." He passed the boat to Callie. "You do the eyes."

With a thin brush she painted an eye shape on each side of the prow in black and gave the eyes blue irises and black pupils.

"They do this in Greece," she said as she painted. "so the fishing boats can find their way home. I saw some on holiday once. I never thought I'd be doing it."

She set the boat down on her desk. It looked beautiful and very fragile.

"Did you get the thread?"

"Yes." She pulled it out of a pocket and tied one end to the boat. "And I've got a penknife for the blood."

"And the Winter King has the Kingfisher feather."

There was a short, weighty silence.

"Then we're ready. And we should go and tell him."

"Yes." Josh got up from the floor and frowned as he did so. "Snow's on again."

Callie turned to look out of the window. The sky had darkened and fat white flakes like feathers were floating lazily down.

"Definitely time we went."

They left the boat on the desk and went downstairs.

"We're going to take Luath out for a walk before it gets any worse," Callie said to George, who was making a pot of soup. "I thought I'd show Josh where mum and dad live."

"All right. Wrap up warm and be back in an hour or your grandmother will fret."

Callie found a pair of wellies that more or less fitted Josh and they piled on their clothes.

"There'll be some hiking boots and a ski jacket at the other house that you can borrow," she said, looking at his rather inadequate layers.

She called Luath and they stepped out into the frozen white world of the front garden. Their breath plumed out in front of them and their feet crunched into the frozen snow.

Just like the dream, Josh thought.

They passed a couple of people pointlessly shovelling snow from their paths, who said hello, but otherwise the village was quiet. There were lights on in the shop though, and through the window they could see the owners clearing spoiled food out of their freezer.

The clouds had covered the sun now, and the snow was coming down faster. Luath kept close to Callie's side, ears pricked, nose working.

"He's a bit twitchy, isn't he?" asked Josh.

"Mmmn ... he can smell something. Maybe it's where the Winterbringers have been." They had passed trickles of sand half-covered by new snow here and there, which Luath had sniffed at tentatively, but quickly backed away from.

They turned down the road to the beach. If you looked carefully, you could still see a trace of tyre tracks from last night. It all seemed dream-like to Josh now, and very long ago. He would hardly find it surprising, he thought, if there was no sign of the Winter King in Callie's house.

He *was* still there though: asleep on the sofa with an arm over his face to shield it from the light.

They stood in the doorway and looked at him properly. Their other encounters with him had been in the cave, or at night. They really hadn't had a chance to see him clearly.

All his clothes, including his boots, seemed to be made of animal skin, and the dyed pattern of blues and greys swirled across it like mist or clouds. There were intricate patterns of stitching: spirals and waves and bird shapes, embellished with mosaic-pieces of shell and bone, which seemed to move and sway as though the sea was caught there.

"Hello?" Callie said uncertainly and he moved his arm away from his face and squinted at them then sat up slowly, as though it took a great effort. His skin was pale as bone and his grey eyes were the colour of the North Sea in winter. He looked unutterably weary. With an effort, he pushed his hair with its braided bones and feathers back from his face and waited for them to speak.

"We've made a boat like the one Agnes described and we think we know where the stream is. When should we try to do this?"

"Now. She is close to death. I feel it. And soon I will be too weak to be of any help."

"Now. All right." Josh swallowed. "Just let me get this jacket I'm meant to be borrowing."

He went out to the hall with Callie and found the jacket and a pair of hiking boots.

"Do you think he'll manage to walk that far?" he asked Callie.

"He doesn't look as if he will. But it matters so much to him ... Look at the weather now though. That's not going to help."

Outside the window there was nothing to be seen but a confusion of flying white flakes.

When they went back in, Luath was sitting at the Winter King's feet, his head on his knee. The King played absently with the dog's ears. Callie opened her mouth to speak and the lights went out.

"Not again!" She went to the window and looked out. There were no lights to be seen. "I think we'd better go while we can," she said, turning back to the others.

They found another jacket for the King to wear to hide the oddness of his clothes as they went through the village.

"Though I doubt there'll be anyone out but us," Callie said grimly.

13. BLIZZARD

They stepped into the blizzard. At once, snow caught on Josh's eyelashes, flew into his ears and mouth. He tugged the hood of his borrowed jacket as far forward as he could and huddled into it.

For a moment, he was completely disoriented, nothing but flying flakes in every direction, Callie's coat a dark blur at his side. The King stood bare-headed in the snow in front of them, Luath beside him, squinting towards the beach.

"They are coming. I feel them making themselves, freeing their bodies from the ice. We must hurry. I am too weak to control them now. They will be here soon."

They didn't bother to ask who he meant.

They crossed the road so they could keep the wall at their side to prevent them from straying in the blinding whiteout, and groped their way along. Every time Josh tried to open his mouth to speak, flakes poured into it. He gave up for the time being and stumbled forward in silence.

A noise like sighing came from over the wall, from among the snow laden-trees beyond it. Josh saw Callie's head whip round as she heard it, saw the King pause and frown, heard Luath start to whimper. It was as though the snow had started to breathe.

"The Black Winter begins to wake," said the King quietly. "The deep cold, the endless cold, is stirring."

There was no sound but the whisper of falling snow and the intermittent sighing from within the trees. Callie felt the hair rise on the back of her neck. At the moment she wanted nothing more than to be past the wood and back in the proper human surroundings of the village.

They tried to quicken their pace, but there was nearly six inches of snow now and the ground near the wall was uneven underneath it. They stumbled forward, Luath pressed against the King's legs.

There was a new sound. A creaking, cracking sound. Josh, who was last out of the three of them, looked back. It was difficult to be sure through the whirl of snowflakes, but he thought he could see two figures, tall and shining, about fifty metres behind them.

"Winterbringers!" he yelled to the others.

Callie turned and squinted into the snow. The King walked back to where Josh was.

"Go on ahead," he said.

"But you're too weak."

"There are only two of them. I can deal with that number. I can send them back into the sea. Go on ahead."

There didn't seem any point arguing, and Josh certainly didn't want to be at the back of the group if there were Winterbringers behind him.

"Luath, come here!" Callie called. The dog turned his head and looked at her, but made no move to leave the King's side.

"Leave him! He won't come." Josh caught Callie's gloved hand and they struggled forward together.

Behind them, the Winter King held his ground, watching the Winterbringers approach. He stooped briefly to pick up a handful of snow, stared at it thoughtfully for a few seconds, then blew on it.

The flakes floated out of his hand and hovered in mid air like a flock of tiny white birds, then began to shape themselves into something. A few seconds later a sword of ice hung in the air before him.

The King curled his hand around the hilt and smiled grimly. "Come closer," he muttered to himself, "and see how weak I am."

The ice creatures had been approaching steadily and now were no more than ten metres away. They looked at him out of faces that were like a crude copy of his own, with the same wide cheek bones and curved nose, but their eyes were blank and white like those of statues. Ears flat, Luath began to growl.

Callie pulled Josh to a stop and turned to look back. They watched helplessly as the Winterbringers closed the distance between them and the King. Even if they had started back towards him they couldn't have got there in time.

One of the Winterbringers reached a heavy hand towards the King. Luath barked and barked and rushed, snapping, at the figures. The sword swung, and swung again. There was an explosion of ice and a strange, high keening sound and for a moment the King was lost from sight among a fountain of ice crystals. Then they cleared and Josh and Callie saw that he had fallen to his knees. In one hand, something glittered.

They started back to help him, but by the time they reached him, he had clambered to his feet. Around him on the snow were shards of ice and shells and trails of weed. In his hand was an impossible sword, a sword made of ice. Luath pressed himself against his leg.

"Keep going," he shouted at them and they turned and started back towards the centre of the village again.

For the moment, nothing seemed to be pursuing them, but the eerie sighing noise still came from within the woods at intervals.

They reached the junction without further incident and turned along past the church. They could only see a few feet in front of them, and no one else seemed to be on the streets, though Callie was half expecting to see George, come to find them. They came to the end of the church wall and fought their way through the snow across to Smithy Road.

It was almost impossible to speak. Josh clung to Callie's hand as though it was the only real object in his world. Close behind, the Winter King and Luath walked together, the ice sword shaking slightly in the King's grip.

"It's there again," Callie said in Josh's ear.

"What is?"

"The net of lights." She pointed. "You still don't see them?"

He shook his head.

The four of them stood side by side in the road.

"Who has woven the net?"

"You see it?"

"Of course." He looked at her as though it was a ridiculous question. "Few now have the power for a making like that." Callie was going to ask what he meant, but before she could he went on. "I do not have the power to break it any more. I cannot pass through."

"But the boat's in there. We have to get it."

"You two can cross, but not me. This net is woven to keep out everything from the Frozen Lands. I cannot pass through it. I will stay outside the wall and wait for you."

"Okay. We'll only be a few minutes. Come on Luath. Time you went in." Luath stood his ground beside the King, paying no heed to his mistress's voice. "Luath, come! Come here dog, we're in a hurry."

She put a hand through Luath's collar to pull him away, but he bared his teeth at her and gave a soft growl.

Astonished, she let go and stepped back, staring. "Luath ...?" she said uncertainly.

"Perhaps you should let him wait here," said the King gently.

Callie nodded, frowning, and turned with Josh to the gate. He pushed it open and they walked across the untrodden snow of the garden – the path completely obscured – to the front door.

Callie let them in and shut pulled the door shut behind them. They stood still, letting their eyes adjust to the presence of colours other than white and the absence of motion.

"Maybe we can get in and out without anyone knowing we're here," said Josh. "It would be a lot easier."

They crept to the bottom of the stairs just as the smithy door opened and Rose came out.

"I'm glad to see you. I was starting to think you'd managed to get lost in the snow. I think your mum's a bit concerned too Josh. You should go through and tell her you're back."

"Oh ... er ... right. I didn't want to mess up the carpets with my boots."

"You could always take them off," said Rose, suppressing a smile. "Where's Luath?"

"He's still outside. I left him in the lane. He's having such a good time in the snow. We just came back for a ball for him. We're going out again – just into the field round the back."

Rose frowned. "Are you sure? It's terribly cold – you both look cold already – and I don't want anything to happen to you."

Callie's voice was smooth as silk. "What could happen Rose? It's snow, just snow." Their gazes caught like magnets, then pulled apart. "You go and say hello to your mother Josh, and I'll get the ball."

He padded off obediently down the dim hall while Callie disappeared upstairs. When he opened the smithy door, a wall of heat and light hit him. The fire was roaring up the chimney, the kitten was curled on the rug, and at least a dozen candles burned in jam jars around the room. It looked like the most perfect sanctuary from everything that was happening outside; he longed to stay, knowing he couldn't. He spent a couple of minutes reassuring his mum and talking to George, then shut the door reluctantly on the glowing warmth.

Callie waited impatiently as he laced his boots again.

"Are you sure you've got everything?" he asked.

Callie shot him a warning glance. Rose, in the kitchen, would be able to hear what they said.

"Yes. I've got the ball and my gloves," she said carefully. "See you in a bit Rose."

Even in that short time indoors they had forgotten how bad it was outside and the whirling chaos of snow took them aback once again. It seemed even colder now, but that was probably after the relative warmth of the house.

They walked through the gate and felt the cold intensify immediately. The snow lay in drifts against the lane wall, freezing as soon as it landed. The wind was like a blade cutting at their skin. They pulled their scarves over their noses and mouths and walked back up the lane to where they had left Luath and the Winter King.

It didn't look as if they'd moved since Josh and Callie last saw them. Little drifts had formed against the King's feet and Luath's paws, and as he saw Callie the dog shook himself free of the snow that had gathered on his coat.

No snow lay on the King. It was as though the flakes slid around him as he stood, the ice sword dangling from his right hand, and heaped themselves round his feet.

"You have the boat?" he said.

Callie nodded and took it from her pocket to show him.

He nodded, mouth curving in what was almost a smile. "It is well made. Perhaps with this we can reach the Kingdom. Which way is the river?"

Callie pointed. "This way; but it's hardly a river – it's hardly even a stream. I only hope it's the right one."

They set off up the lane to go round the back of the garden and over the fields to the tiny stream. Callie watched the sparkling threads of light in the air above the Smithy. She had no idea why Josh couldn't see them or what the King had meant when he had asked who had woven the net, and there seemed no time to ask now.

As they moved away from the Smithy garden and into the field they began to hear the breath of the Black Winter around them. Despite their layers of clothing, Josh and Callie were both shivering, although the King seemed impervious to the cold.

The constant blowing of white flakes in front of his eyes made Josh feel dizzy and disoriented. He wanted to stop and sit down and close his eyes, just for a moment, to get some rest from them.

Luath began to bark just then and suddenly a figure loomed out of the snow in front of them: a shining figure, like a copy in ice of the Winter King, every detail right now, even as it was so terribly wrong.

"Stay behind me!" he said to Josh and Callie and waited for the Winterbringer to come to him. Josh noticed that it moved more swiftly and fluidly than any of the others they had seen. It was as though each one was a better copy than the one before.

This one was careful to keep out of reach of the sword, circling the King like a grotesque mirror image. It was only when Luath threw himself at the creature, teeth bared, that it paused, distracted, for long enough to let the King lunge forward and drive the sword into its body in a shower of crystals.

The sword fell from his hand and Josh bent to pick it up.

"Careful! The cold will burn you."

"Even through gloves?" They were thick ski gloves.

"I do not know. Be careful."

Josh picked the sword up gingerly. He felt the cold pour from it into his hand, and passed it quickly to the King.

"I am sorry. I must rest for a few moments," he said and slipped to his knees.

"That's all right. I could do with a rest too." Josh sat down dizzily in the snow, his hands over his face, seeking relief from the endless unbroken whiteness around them.

Callie knelt down beside them. "Just for a moment," she said, anxiety clear in her voice. "We mustn't fall asleep. We could freeze."

"How could anyone fall asleep in this?" asked Josh.

Around them the snow breathed, slow and menacing.

⁂

Callie felt something warm and wet against her face, between her scarf and hat. She recognized it as Luath's tongue and pushed him away, wondering how he'd managed to get into her bedroom. She felt for the edge of the duvet, to pull it further up. There was no duvet. She realized slowly where she was and opened her eyes to see Luath licking at Josh's face where he lay curled in the snow a few feet away from her.

She moved, stiff with cold, her brain working painfully slowly. She knew they had to get up and move or they would die here of the cold. She saw Josh push the dog away and crawled across to him. Luath transferred his efforts to the Winter King, who knelt bare-headed in the snow, still as a statue, the sword fallen from his grip, eyes open but empty.

Josh pushed himself onto his hands and knees, shaking his head to try and clear it.

Callie got painfully to her feet and helped Josh to pull himself up.

"How long ..." he started to say.

She pulled her glove down far enough to see her watch. "Five minutes, maybe ten."

"We could have died."

"I know." She gave an involuntary shudder.

They pushed through the mounds of snow to the King and hauled him to his feet.

"I hope the river is close," he said as Josh handed the sword to him again. "I cannot go much further."

"It's not far," said Callie. "Just down ..." She looked around, unsure of what way she was facing. "Wait a minute." She looked around for their tracks, but the snow had already blotted them out. *Think,* she said to herself in her head. *Concentrate.* She looked up this time, hoping to see the glimmer of lights over the Smithy. At first there was nothing but snow. She turned slowly, watching carefully.

There.

She kept looking for a minute to make sure, then turned away from the Smithy lights.

"Down there." She pointed into the blurred snow.

"Are you sure?" said Josh, doubtfully.

"Yes." She certainly sounded sure.

They fought their way forward. Around them the wind rose higher, blowing snow so hard at them that it was virtually impossible to speak. Above the wind came the loud breath of the Black Winter, deeper and faster now, like an animal rousing from sleep.

They pushed on as fast as they could, but now the snow seemed to fight them at every step. Callie wasn't as sure as she had sounded that she was heading in the right direction, so it was with enormous relief that she saw through the blizzard the line of small trees that marked the river bank.

"There!" she yelled at Josh.

He nodded in return.

"Nearly there," she shouted encouragingly to the King.

With a sound like shattering glass, the fallen snow around them exploded into life.

14. Summer's Heart

Hands shot out of the icy snow around them, grabbing sightlessly. Too shocked to scream or run, Josh and Callie froze.

Arms emerged fully, shoulders, heads, dragging themselves from the frozen mounds of snow, each one a replica of the Winter King, their icy hair woven with feathers and bones of frost.

"Run!" yelled the King. "Get to the river. See to the boat. You cannot help here."

Luath ran here and there, biting at hands and faces as they emerged, maiming but not killing the ice creatures.

"Go!"

They turned and ran for the river as best they could, swerving, half-falling; anything to avoid the grasping hands. They crashed through the trees in a shower of snow and there lay the stream in front of them, frozen solid.

Callie pulled the boat out of her pocket and set it down on the ice. The thread had already been fastened to it in the Smithy. Josh pulled off his gloves with his teeth and willed his numb fingers to tie the other end round an alder branch which Callie showed him.

"Nothing's happening," he said anxiously.

"The blood," Callie yelled in his ear. "We forgot the blood."

They glanced back up the slope, to where the Winter King and Luath held the ice-warriors at bay.

Callie fumbled for the penknife in her pocket and tried unsuccessfully to open it.

"Give it to me."

She passed it to Josh without argument. He blew on his fingers and pulled at the blade and it slowly unfolded. He jabbed the point into his thumb immediately and passed it back to Callie and held his hand over the boat on the ice. His fingers were so cold that the blood wouldn't flow out of the cut. He rubbed his thumb hard with his other hand, coaxed a sullen drop from it and let it fall into the boat.

Up on the bank, the King and Luath were retreating before the onslaught of the ice warriors, one slow step at a time.

Callie let her blood fall into the boat, her breath held.

Nothing happened.

"What's wrong?" she yelled. "We did everything. Why isn't it working?"

"I don't know."

They stared at the boat as though they could will it to do what they wanted.

Think, Callie urged herself. *Picture Agnes' journal. Remember the words.*

Beatrix had a long coil of white silk thread. She tied one end to the boat and the other to a trailing branch, so the boat would find its way home, then set it down on the water of the ...

"The water!"

"What?"

"The boat has to be on the water. Quick, we have to break the ice."

Luath and the King had fallen back to the trees now. They only had a few more seconds before they would all be overwhelmed. Josh and Callie kicked at the snow on the bank trying to find something they could use to break the ice. With a gasp, Josh pulled a fist-sized stone free from the earth and hammered at the ice in front of the boat.

"Hurry!" screamed Callie "They're coming."

Josh struck at the ice over and over again, as hard as he could, but it didn't even crack.

"It's no good."

With a sob, Callie threw herself at the ice and hammered at it with her fists.

"Break! Break!"

The ice shattered under her hand and split apart, a channel of shining dark water opening in front of the tiny boat. The slab of ice it lay on tilted sideways and the boat slid down and onto the water.

As they watched, it seemed to shiver, and then to swell, until it lay tethered by a white rope to the tree, a small boat still, but big enough for all of them.

Callie threw herself into the boat and held tight to a branch to stop it drifting.

"Quick – get in!" Josh yelled.

Luath bounded down the bank and jumped into the boat.

With a cry, the Winter King hurled the ice sword at the Winterbringers. It shattered into tiny shards with a noise like a bell and he fell and rolled down the slope.

Josh hauled him into the boat and half-fell in himself and Callie pushed off.

As well as the boat, the stream seemed to have grown much wider and within a few seconds they were floating in a channel in the centre, out of reach of anything on the bank.

Josh pulled himself up and looked properly at the boat. "It worked," he said in amazement, staring at the reddish-brown stains on the bottom. "What did you do to the ice?"

"I didn't do any thing to it. I just hit it."

"But I'd been hammering it with that stone and nothing had happened."

"I must just have hit a weak spot or something. I don't know. It doesn't matter anyway."

"No." He turned to the King. "Are you all right?"

The King nodded, still gasping for breath as he lay in the bottom of the boat, one hand clutching the pouch at his throat that held the precious feather.

On the shore, the ice warriors moved, scenting the air like dogs, but unwilling or unable to enter the water.

The ice drew apart before the boat as it moved smoothly through the water, and the stream widened and settled within steeply cut banks as the white rope uncoiled behind them.

Callie looked back, but there was only an indistinct milky white mist.

The boat moved steadily on, as though it had a purpose. Luath had moved to the prow with Callie and sat eagerly, head up, ears pricked, sniffing the unfamiliar air.

Trees leaned in above them, bare branches strung with tiny icicles arching and lacing together above the stream so that they slid through a still, silvery tunnel.

"Where are we?" Josh breathed.

"Wherever we are, we're not in Pitmillie any more."

"We are on the path to the Kingdom of Summer," said the King softly from behind her, sitting up and looking around him properly for the first time since he tumbled into the boat. "If it still exists at all." He pulled off his borrowed jacket and dropped it in the bottom of the boat.

His words were ominous and indeed, there was no trace of summer in the landscape around them.

They sat in silence as the boat sailed on through its channel.

"The ice is getting thinner," said Josh suddenly. The others looked for a moment.

"You're right," said Callie.

Above them, the sky began to change. The snow clouds thinned and dissolved and were replaced by the sun, low in the sky, turning the tunnel of trees and the boat golden.

The icicles had gone from the branches and instead a few dead leaves clung to them, brown-gold. The ice had receded to the thinnest of crusts at the edge of the stream and the water flowed smoothly, as though it was deep. Here and there the surface was dotted with the shrivelled remains of water plants.

Time passed. They drifted wordlessly through a landscape that had changed from winter not to summer, but to autumn: a landscape of brown and yellow, silver-grey and gold. A dying landscape, Callie thought, rousing from a dream. She had no idea how long they had been in the boat.

Before them now, the stream widened to a still pool. At the far side was a little jetty of silvery wood, overgrown with moss and lichen. Moored to it was a boat, much like their own, with a coil of white rope in the bottom. Josh and Callie stared at it, wide-eyed.

"Do you think ..." Callie started to say.

"It can't be, can it?"

Their voices sounded appallingly loud against the silence that enveloped the place.

"Agnes said the boat went back," she went on in a whisper. "But that was over three hundred years ago. It couldn't still be here. It looks as new as ours."

"Agnes said that time seemed to forget what to do here," mused Josh.

The boat drew itself up alongside the jetty and stopped. Josh and Callie turned to the King, not sure what to do next. His face was unreadable as he climbed wearily from the boat. There was no sound, no sign of a living creature, only the trees ahead of them, hung with rags of autumn leaves, and a winding path of dry brown grass that twisted away through them.

The others climbed onto the jetty, and Luath took his place at the King's side again. At the edge of the jetty the King hesitated for a moment, then set his foot to the grass and started along the path, the others behind him.

The way led through groves of trees, some of which Callie, though not Josh, recognized as oak and rowan and birch. Others were unfamiliar to her. Many were dead, branches stark against the sky, and the others looked as they would at the end of autumn, stubborn remnants of leaves clinging to the branches here and there.

Their feet moved through heaps of fallen leaves that no breeze had stirred, as they followed the path up a slope, the King leading the way with Luath at his side, Callie and Josh behind.

Below them lay a broad valley covered in tussocky dry grass and tangled brambles, bare of leaves. The low rays of the sun stained some of them a rusty red, as though they were bleeding, or burning.

In the middle of the valley was a tremendous twisted snarl of tree trunks and shrubs, branches sprouting from it at odd angles, fungi clamped to trunks like great brackets, ivy choking everything.

The King gave a cry of anguish.

They looked at his stricken face.

"What is this place?" asked Josh.

"It is her palace," he replied with difficulty. "Summer's heart."

"Oh, Agnes," whispered Callie, "what did you do?"

Josh and Callie stared, trying to reconcile the bleak scene in front of them with Agnes' description of the Queen of Summer's palace, with its walls of birch and roses and honeysuckle, all leaf and blossom, pierced with doorways and windows. There was no sign of a doorway in this tangle of dying wood before them.

"Are we too late?" Callie's voice shook.

"I do not know. I fear it when I see this place, and yet I cannot believe that she could die and I not know it. We must go down and find a way in. If she still lives, that is where she will be."

They began to pick their way down the slope, treacherous with dead leaves and twisted, grasping stems of grass, zig-zagging to avoid clumps of bramble. Callie thought she had never been in such a melancholy place in her life. There was no sound – not a note of birdsong or an insect's buzz – just the noise of leaves and snapping stems under their wary feet.

They reached the bottom of the slope and made their way across the floor of the valley to the remains of the palace. Their was no obvious way in, nothing that resembled a door or window. They followed the King's lead and began to tear at the ivy that cloaked most of this side of the palace in great sour-smelling swathes. Watching him from the corner of her eye as they pulled it down, Callie realized that he had regained some strength since they reached the Kingdom, even in its present, ruinous state. At that moment, Josh yelled.

"Here. I think there's a way in."

You certainly couldn't have called it a doorway. It was just a narrow gap between two huge briar stems that seemed to lead, reasonably straight, through the whole living thickness of the wall.

He squeezed and twisted his way through, Callie following. The King, being taller and broader, had more difficulty, but no barrier would have stopped him now, and he emerged a few seconds later, scratched and panting. Luath loped in behind him, and they turned to see what lay inside the palace.

Brambles and ivy had laced hands across much of the roof opening, and it took their eyes a few seconds to adjust to the dimness. When they did, the first thing they saw was a dead, white tree in the centre of the great hall in which they stood, split as though struck by lightning. Most of the floor was bare earth, but here and there clumps of grass were still green, and there were a few, a very few, tiny white and golden flowers among them.

"Oh no; the poor things." Callie was close to tears; the King beyond speech.

Here and there on the ground were the bodies of dragonflies and birds and butterflies, a few still moving, but close to death. They moved among them, sick and silent with fear, but nowhere did they find the body of a Kingfisher; and then the King gave a cry and reached his hand inside the split trunk of the birch tree and brought out something greeny-blue and chestnut, that he held as though it was indescribably precious.

"Is ..." Josh couldn't bear to have his question answered.

The King sank to his knees, cradling the Kingfisher in his left hand as he reached for the pouch around his neck with the other. In his hand, the bird lay quite still and limp. He brought out the feather and laid it on the Kingfisher's breast and held the bird between his two hands.

"Do not be dead, my love," he whispered. "See; I have brought you back yourself. You are whole again. Do not be dead."

15. The Queen of Summer

Callie's eyes clouded with tears that she made no move to wipe away. The King and the Kingfisher were indistinct in her blurred sight, seeming to shimmer and move and change. She blinked the tears away and drew her breath in sharply and was still, Josh at her side staring too at what was before them.

On his knees, the King cradled a woman in his arms. Her dress was a shifting pattern of blue-green and chestnut overlaid with veins of gold. Her hair, spilling over the King's arms and on to the ground, was sunlight and rose petals and ripe oats and streamers of cloud. Her eyes, when they opened, were the blue of a summer night.

The Winter King and the Queen of Summer each held the other in their gaze, drinking in the presence they had each thought they would never see again.

After what seemed like a very long time, the Queen spoke.

"What have you done? I am whole. How have you done this?"

It seemed he would never speak, that he could not have his fill of simply looking at her, but finally he said,

"I came from the Frozen Lands one final time to be with you when you died and the Black Winter overwhelmed the land, but these two" – he drew her gaze to Josh and Callie – "found what had been taken from you, so long ago. It is they who have saved you."

"I do not understand this," she said wonderingly, "but there will be time for that." She smiled. "Now, there will be time."

Around the hall the creatures who had lain dying a few minutes ago stirred, and shifted between bird or insect and human form. Those that were dead however, did not change.

As their human forms settled about them they sat and stared, marvelling, at their Queen, who seemed to grow stronger by the second.

She sat up fully now, and indicated Luath. "And who is this?"

"This is my noble companion Luath, who helped me slay many ice warriors who would have stopped us reaching you. Without him I do not think I could have withstood them."

The King stood and drew her to her feet, and she walked, leaning on him a little, to where Josh and Callie and Luath waited.

The Queen held one of Josh's hands between her own and stared into his eyes for a few seconds. He had to make an effort to meet her gaze, for it was as though she could see straight into his heart. She smiled and let go, then turned to Callie and cupped her cheek in her hand. Her smile widened. "You, I recognize," she said.

"But I've never seen you before."

"True; but you are like the other one."

Callie was silent, puzzled.

Lastly, the Queen put a hand under Luath's muzzle and tilted his head up so that they could look at each other. "Thank you," she said to the dog gravely.

She turned back to the King. The remains of her people were gathering about her now, communicating, somehow, without speech.

The Queen looked about her at the ruins of her palace. "There is much to do, but in time the Kingdom of Summer will be as it was before." She turned back to Josh and Callie. "And your land will be as it should, but you will have to be patient, for it will take a long time for the seasons to regain their balance. It may be years, by your reckoning."

She looked thoughtful. "You should go back now. I do not know how long you have been here."

Her words struck a chill through Callie. She remembered the Queen's words in Agnes' journal. *Who knows how much time may have passed while you have been here?*

"Yes, of course we should. Come on, Luath." This time the dog came to her side straight away.

The King came forward and put a hand on each of their shoulders. "Callie ... Josh ... There is nothing I can say that is enough. You found me in despair, dying; you have restored to me my life and my love, and yet there is nothing I can give you in thanks, for it is certainly clear that nothing of the Kingdom of Summer may go into your world again."

"But the Queen said our world is mended too. That seems like pretty good thanks to me," said Josh.

The King nodded, smiling.

⁂

A little later, Josh, Callie and Luath stood at the top of the slope looking back down to the overgrown palace. Already the Queen's people were at work hauling down great sheets of ivy and bramble. They had uncovered one of the windows so that the palace was no longer blind.

The King and Queen stood together just outside, watching them go, and they raised their hands in farewell. Josh and Callie waved and turned to walk through the woods back to the boat.

At first they were silent, trying to digest what had happened, but as they took in properly what was around them, Callie spoke.

"How could that happen so quickly?"

The last of the dead leaves had fallen and in their place, green buds were breaking from every tree and bush.

Josh shook his head. "I've got no idea. I just hope it *has* happened quickly."

They increased their pace, anxious now to get back to where they belonged, Luath trotting ahead. As they emerged from the woods, Callie stopped so abruptly that Josh crashed into her.

"It's gone," she said.

With a sick feeling in the pit of his stomach, Josh looked at the jetty and the pool beyond. There was no trace of their boat, tethered to their own world by its white rope. Only Agnes' boat lay at rest in the water.

"We didn't tell it to wait. Agnes said they told their boat to wait. We forgot to do that," she said, panic mounting in her voice.

"It's okay," Josh said, trying to sound calm. "We'll just go back and get them to help us make a boat. It won't be hard; after all there's plenty of wood."

"But that will take time, and we've no idea how long we've really been here."

But Josh had thought of something worse. "We can't," he said, his voice flat. "Remember? Nothing from the Kingdom can go into our world again."

"But we can send it back."

"Can you see them risking that after what's just happened?"

"No."

There was a despondent silence.

"We'll just have to take Agnes' boat and hope it remembers the way home."

"It's three hundred years old! It must be falling to bits."

"It doesn't look as though it's falling to bits. And at least it comes from our world. Do you have a better idea?"

He sighed. "No. I don't have any ideas."

"Well, then."

As though he had been waiting for the end of the discussion, Luath jumped neatly down into the boat. It rocked against the jetty and settled again.

Callie got in next and Josh, cautiously, last. The boat seemed perfectly sound.

"Now what?"

There was no mooring rope to untie, no oars to row with.

"Come on boat, do something. You must have worked without oars before. Take us back."

Nothing happened.

Callie tried. "Boat, take us home; back to Pitmillie." She pushed against the jetty to set the boat moving out into the pool.

They held their breath. The boat turned and moved smoothly out across the water towards the river that had brought them here. As it nosed into the channel there was a flash of blue and they looked up to see a pair of Kingfishers swooping around the boat before taking flight through the wood.

Josh and Callie smiled at each other in wonder. "That's them, isn't it?"

Callie nodded. "I think so."

They were moving down the river now, away from the Kingdom. Luath sat with his head on the side of the boat, watching the banks go by. Callie and Josh looked around them more anxiously, seeing everywhere signs of new growth. As the trees closed in around them, stitched with tiny buds, Josh said, "Shouldn't there be ice by now?"

"I'm not sure. Maybe it doesn't start until we're closer to home."

Unfurling leaves of water plants lay on the stream's surface now, where previously there had only been frost-blackened stems.

At last and to their huge relief, there came the first faint cracks as thin ice broke before the boat and the landscape that they could glimpse through the tunnel of trees turned more wintry by the moment. As it did so however, they became aware of another, less welcome change.

"What's happening to the boat?" asked Callie in alarm as a piece of the edge crumbled under her fingers. Luath's hackles rose.

Although it still moved steadily forward, the boat had begun to creak and groan around them.

"I think it's remembered how old it really is," replied Josh, keeping as still as possible.

Around them, the ice was growing thicker, and the boat slowed, having increasing trouble pushing its way through.

"How close are we to Pitmillie?" he called to Callie, as a shudder seemed to pass through the entire boat.

She squinted through the trees on the bank. "Not very far I think. The stream's getting narrower and the banks aren't so steep."

"I hope you're right," he said desperately as the wood began to split.

"There's the other boat!" Callie yelled, and he looked to where she was pointing just as, with a great crack, Agnes Blair's boat fell apart under them, throwing them into the icy stream.

Fortunately it was only hip-deep, though cold enough to take their breath away. They hauled themselves out on the bank just in time to see the last piece of timber, with a faded eye still visible on it, disappear below the surface.

Luath shook the water out of his rough coat, making the two of them even wetter in the process. They stood on the bank, shivering.

"What should we do about our boat?"

"I think we have to send it back like Agnes did," said Callie between chattering teeth. They picked their way along the bank to where their boat lay and untied the rope that tethered it to their world. Josh lifted the Winter King's borrowed jacket from the bottom.

"You should have waited you know," Callie said reproachfully to the boat. "Anyway, you'd better go back now. Off you go."

She pushed the boat away from the bank and watched as a channel opened in front of it through the ice and it moved off.

"Ready?" asked Josh.

She nodded. "Ready."

They pulled each other up the bank and through the trees, hearts thudding. What would they find? How long *had* they been in the Kingdom of Summer?

In front of them, the fields still lay white, but the snow clouds had piled away into the north and pale sunlight gilded the snow. More than that: it was *warm* sunlight, and when they listened they could hear steady dripping as the snow and ice began to melt, but that was all; the snow itself was silent.

They set off towards the Smithy as fast as they could and Callie gave a gasp of relief when it came into view, still with the net of lights in the sky above it.

"Can you see them now?"

"Are you still seeing lights?" Josh squinted up at the sky above the house, shading his eyes with a hand. "Nope. Still nothing. It can't just be your eyes though. The King saw them too. What was it he said?"

"Few now have the power for a making like that." Callie

stopped dead. "I think it was Agnes. Maybe some of the power from that feather rubbed off on her and she was able to do it."

"Don't you think you'd have noticed them before, in that case?" He shivered. "Come on, I'm too cold to stand still."

They started to walk again.

"Maybe it was like a sort of burglar alarm, and it took the Winterbringers to set it off."

"Mmmn ... Still doesn't explain why I can't see it."

"Maybe something from the feather got into me when I had the box in my bedroom."

Josh looked at her sidelong. "It all sounds a bit far fetched."

"And what we've just done doesn't?"

"I'm too cold to care about lights any more. Come on."

They ran the rest of the way, in an agony of uncertainty. Everything looked as it should, but the building probably looked more or less the same as it had done in Agnes' time and as it would in another three hundred years.

Half frozen, they shoved open the gate, Luath barking with joy to be home. Callie fumbled for her keys but before she could find them the front door opened and Rose was looking at them in horror.

"You're soaked! What happened? And where on earth have you been? You know you've been gone more than two hours? George has been out looking for you."

Josh and Callie looked at each other and burst out laughing.

16. JUSTICE

The power eventually came back on at ten o'clock that night, and it looked as though, this time, it might stay on. Other places weren't so lucky, however. As they watched the news reports that seemed to be almost the only thing on television just now, they realized that compared with the rest of the country they'd missed the worst of the weather.

There was footage of huge snowdrifts that had swallowed up whole houses in Wales, and fishing boats locked in frozen harbours all round the coast. Thousands of people were still without electricity, and the thaw that was now well underway seemed certain to make things worse before they got better, with forecasts of flooding in many areas.

Anna's mobile went while they were watching. "Susan? Hello? I can hardly hear you. Where are you?" Everyone else in the room could hear a loud throbbing coming from the phone. Anna went out of the room to take the rest of the call.

When she came back in she looked worried again.

"What's going on, mum? Where's Susan?"

"She was calling from our kitchen."

"What? But that noise ..."

Anna sighed. "It's very good of them really ...

They've organized a company to put dehumidifiers in our flat to dry it out. That's what you heard. They're there for another three days. All the time. Twenty four hours."

"We can't go back there. We'll never sleep."

"I know, but what else can we do?"

"Stay here," said Rose. "You don't have to spend the time talking to us, you know. I know you've got your book to finish. Spread yourself out in the dining room and have a couple of days of peace and quiet and I'll bet you find it doesn't take as long to finish as you think. Now that the heating's back on you should be quite comfortable in there."

She hadn't needed much persuading and was in there by seven the next morning, books and papers and photos spread all over the big table.

Everyone else slept late, the tension that had wound them up for the last few days suddenly gone. The house was unwarded now, for Rose had let the lights die with the night, knowing without understanding the reason, that the danger was past. She couldn't rid herself of an unreasonable suspicion that Josh and Callie knew something about it, although that was plainly ridiculous.

Bessie phoned that morning.

"What did you do, you clever girl?"

"I didn't do anything," Rose replied.

"But it's gone. It *has* gone, hasn't it?"

"Yes. The world feels normal again, but I don't know why and that bothers me. I keep thinking it's got something to do with Callie, but I know it can't have."

"You don't know that at all. You're not even sure if

she has the Gift. For all you know, she does and she was strong enough to do this on her own."

"Don't be ridiculous," Rose spluttered. "I would know."

There was silence on the other end of the phone.

"Bessie? Are you still there?"

"You're going to have to talk to her sometime."

Rose sighed. "I know. But I promised her mother I wouldn't do it while she was away. You know she would prefer it if I never spoke to Callie about it at all."

"Do you think it would have been different if she'd had the Gift herself?"

"I doubt it. She always hated the fact that I did. She used to try to pretend it wasn't real. I think it frightened her – still does, in fact."

Bessie gave a snort. "Well, I'm glad that's your problem, not mine.

"Anyway, it doesn't really matter if we understand what happened, does it? After all, we're just four eccentric old dears in most people's eyes. What'll we find to worry about now?" mused Bessie.

"Oh, I'm sure we'll soon find something," Rose said, smiling.

She and George were busy in the garden for most of the day, trying to salvage plants that were never meant to have been exposed to such extreme temperatures.

To George's joy, the bees seemed to have survived unscathed. Josh watched, fascinated, from what he hoped was a safe distance, as he fed the hive with a mixture of sugar and water.

Josh and Callie had stayed up late into the night,

talking about what had happened; trying to fix it in their memories, for already it seemed to be melting a little with the thaw, becoming indistinct round the edges. They looked out of the windows as they spoke, watching for any signs of Winterbringers, any sound of breathing snow, but the world seemed to be remembering how to behave, and the only sound was of water dripping constantly as the snowy landscape thawed around them.

On the way back from the bees in search of a cup of tea, George suddenly said, "I've kept forgetting to ask, with everything that's been going on: did you ever manage to open that box you found up the smithy chimney?"

They'd realized that someone would eventually ask.

"Yes," Callie replied. "I meant to tell you, but, you know ..." She made a gesture that encompassed the snow and Josh and life in general.

"What was in it?"

"Just some letters. Well, not letters exactly: a sort of journal, from ... when was it Josh?"

"Seventeen-oh-something."

"Some girl called Agnes Blair."

George stopped in his tracks. "Really? That's interesting." He went on towards the house without elaborating.

They sat down with tea and huge slices of fruit cake and after five minutes or so, George said, "Let's have a look at the box and this journal then Callie."

Callie brought it down from her room and handed George the bundle of folded papers, then she and Josh went back out to help Rose for a bit longer.

"I thought George was coming back out?" she said.

"He's reading. Remember that box I found up the chimney when Chutney Mary got stuck? Well, it had a sort of diary thing in it from ages ago."

"Goodness, how interesting."

"Not really. It doesn't make sense. I reckon she must have made a lot of it up."

"She?"

"The girl who wrote it – Agnes Blair."

Rose looked up sharply. "Agnes Blair? Now that *is* interesting." And she headed off towards the house without another word.

Callie and Josh looked at each other.

"What was all that about?"

"I've got no idea. But we'd better stay put here for a while. We don't want to look too fascinated after pretending we weren't interested in it." Callie scratched her nose with a muddy hand.

They forced themselves to wait for half an hour, finishing things off and tidying up, before they went back in.

In the kitchen Rose sat at the big table, the open strongbox on the table in front of her and Agnes' journal in her hand. She looked up at them with an unfathomable expression on her face.

"Imagine this being up the chimney all that time." She shook her head and said, a little too casually, "Was there anything else in the box when you opened it?"

Callie gave her a stare of wide-eyed innocence. "No, just that. Why?"

"Oh, I just wondered. No treasure then?"

"No."

"You might find this interesting." Rose pushed a wooden box across the table to Josh and Callie.

Callie picked it up. It looked old, and was heavy for its size, quite plain, apart from a crude letter A carved into the lid. She glanced quickly at Rose, then opened the tarnished brass clasp. Inside was a sheaf of folded papers, much like the ones Rose still held.

She unfolded them and immediately recognized the angular black writing.

"Is this Agnes' too?"

Rose nodded.

"Where did it come from?"

"We found it when we had the central heating put in. It was under the floorboards in your bedroom."

Josh and Callie pulled out chairs and sat down and began to read.

⚘⚘⚘

My name is Agnes Blair and I write this as a record of what happened to my friends Beatrix Laing and Janet Corphat, and what happened to me, so that one day someone will know the truth.

Patrick Morton denounced them as witches to Minister Cowper, a very wicked man, who I think now must simply have hated all women. He saw to it that they were arrested and taken to Pittenweem to be put to the question.

I did not dare to go there, coward that I was, and instead I waited for news of what was happening to make its way back to Pitmillie.

They were kept for days with no sleep and hardly any food, but they kept their wits and admitted nothing. And named no one else. Eventually Cowper tired of his sport and sent to Edinburgh to have them tried at the High Court.

It was nearly five months before they gave him an answer, and all that time Beatrix and Janet were kept in prison and that wicked fool Patrick Morton strutted about preening as though he had done something good.

When the answer came from Edinburgh, it wasn't what Mr Cowper wanted to hear. It said there wasn't the evidence for a trial at the High Court and that he should fine them and let them go.

Beatrix's family paid the fine and she came back to Pitmillie, thinking she could take up her life again, but nobody wanted her there, not even her own relatives. When I heard she was being forced out of the village, I sneaked away from the Smithy with some food for her.

I caught up with her on the road to St Andrews, shouting at her to make her stop.

"Beatrix! Wait! It's Agnes."

She turned round and my heart caught in my throat, she was so changed. Her face was gaunt and her eyes were dead and her hair had turned grey, all in the space of those few months.

"Go away Agnes. I'm tainted. You mustn't be seen talking to me."

"I brought you some food." I thrust a bundle at her, with bread and cheese and apples in it.

She took it and looked at me for a few seconds, as if she was trying to fix my face in her mind, and sighed.

"We meant no harm. We did no harm. We helped them, stupid fools."

She turned and walked away from me and I never saw her again.

*****

What happened to Beatrix was bad enough, but I can hardly bear to write of Janet. The Lords in Edinburgh had said that she should be released too, but she was arrested again as soon as she set foot outside the prison a few days after Beatrix. It was her tongue got her into trouble, as folk had always said it would. She'd ridiculed Cowper when he questioned her and he had determined to take revenge for the injury to his dignity.

He had her flogged, or I should say, flogged her himself, trying to force her into a confession, but she wouldn't give in to him, so he flung her back into jail again, to rot there forever, the folk in Pitmillie said, when the news reached here the next day.

I'd had enough. It was time I stood by my friends as they'd stood by me. I waited until the family were all in bed and safely asleep, then took my father's horse and set out for Pittenweem.

I remember that night so clearly. There wasn't a breath of wind, and the air smelled clean and new and full of spring and green things growing. The moon was almost full, and so bright the horse and I had no trouble finding our way. In no time at all, I was in Pittenweem.

I saw no one as we went silently through the streets. Not a light showed at the fisher cottage windows. I tied the horse a little way from the Tolbooth Jail and crept through the night towards Janet.

Even here the windows were dark, and there seemed to be no guard. I risked sound.

"Janet!" I hissed. "Where are you?"

No answer. I walked round the building a bit and tried again.

"Janet! Answer me. I've come to help."

This time, there was a noise, low down, and after a few seconds a voice spoke, close to my knees.

"Who's there?"

I hardly recognized the weak, cracked voice. I knelt down and saw there was an iron grille in the wall, just above the ground. The moonlight didn't penetrate into the dank dark beyond.

"It's Agnes. Come to the window."

There was a shuffling sound, and then a thin bruised hand grasped one of the bars and I saw Janet's face. Meeting Beatrix had prepared me a little for how changed she'd be, or I would not have known her. I tried to smile.

"Can you get through here if I can get the grille off?"

She nodded.

The grille had a hinge at one side and a lock at the other. I had brought one of my father's hammers with me, the head wrapped in a rag to deaden the sound.

"Stand back," I said and raised the hammer.

Even with the rags it sounded terribly loud. I struck blow after blow at the lock, maybe a dozen in all. Nothing happened.

Janet's face reappeared. "Agnes, you can't do it. Go

away before someone hears you. Beatrix and I tried so hard to keep you safe: I couldn't bear it if you were taken now."

"I'm not leaving you here." I raised the hammer high again and put all my strength behind it. "Break!" I hissed at the lock as I swung it down.

It broke.

I knelt there, stupid with amazement. I'd no idea how I'd done it. I knew I wasn't strong enough to break that lock.

"Agnes?"

Janet's voice brought me back to myself. I hauled open the grille and reached in to help her climb through.

She lay gasping on the ground. In the moonlight I could see the weals on her back through her tattered clothes. I took off my cloak and helped her to her feet and wrapped it round her to hide her rags. She leaned against the corner of the building, catching her breath.

"Come on," I said. "We can't stay here."

"No Agnes. We part here. You've given me my life. You must take the hammer and go home so that no one will ever know what you did. I'll go my own road." She pulled me close and hugged me and kissed me, then released me, grinning so that for a moment she looked almost like the old Janet. "Goodbye. We'll not meet again." She limped off across the street towards a narrow wynd.

I knew she was right, but I hated to leave her like that. I still wonder what would have happened if I'd stayed.

The horse was waiting where I'd left him, and we made our way home through the moonlight and were never seen.

If only that was the end of the story. I went about my chores in Pitmillie, imagining Janet making her slow way to Kirkcaldy perhaps, or Edinburgh, but it wasn't to be.

They found her gone first thing in the morning of course and hunted her down. It was easy for the dogs to find her, because of the smell of the blood from the flogging.

The whole town gathered to see her brought back, but instead of putting her in the Tolbooth again they hauled her down to the beach. They bound her and strung her from a mooring rope between a ship and the shore, and then they stoned her.

They took her down half-dead and threw her on the sand and laid boards on her, and the mob piled stones on top until they had crushed her to death. I believe Mr Cowper watched.

That was Janet Corphat's justice, and it has haunted me all my life.

There is one more thing. About a month after Janet died, Patrick Morton fell ill again, quite suddenly. He did not rave this time. Rather, he seemed to have been struck dumb. I helped nurse him and though he couldn't speak, I could tell from his eyes that he understood what was happening. He died after a few days.

And that was Patrick Morton's justice.

17. AGNES

They sat silent for minutes after they had finished reading, taking in what Agnes had written. Across the table, Rose still held the papers from the strongbox.

"Is this true?" asked Callie finally.

Rose nodded. She looked suddenly old.

"Beatrix Laing and Janet Corphat were accused of witchcraft by a man called Patrick Morton. Beatrix was forced to leave and Janet died just as it says there." She gestured at Agnes' account. "It was all documented at the time. But there's no mention of Agnes Blair being associated with them. Patrick Morton died in seventeen oh five right enough. You can see his gravestone in the churchyard."

We meant no harm. We did no harm. The words went round and round in Callie's head as she thought about Agnes and Beatrix and Janet and Patrick Morton, about the Winter King and the Queen of Summer and what they had all had to endure because of that one midsummer night, more than three hundred years ago.

"I wonder what happened to Agnes in the end?" mused Josh.

"She married and had children and died in her bed an old woman," said Rose unexpectedly. "She's buried over the road as well." She took a deep breath and plunged on.

"You're related to her, Callie. She's your great great something grandmother. Mine too."

Callie stared at the black writing in front of her, trying to take everything in.

"I think I'll put all this away now," said Rose, and took the papers from her and folded them up.

⁂

"Well, that's everything," said Anna. "I'm sure you've given us enough fruit and veg to last us until Christmas."

"No we haven't," laughed George. "So come back for some more before then."

The car was loaded up and the engine was running. Josh and Callie stood awkwardly side by side as the others said their goodbyes.

"Well Josh," Rose said to him. "I hope you didn't find village life too boring?"

"Eh ... no. Definitely not boring. Thanks for everything."

They all walked to the car and Josh and Anna climbed in. Josh opened his window.

Callie summoned a smile. "Bye, then. Bet you'll be glad to get back to a normal life."

He screwed up his face. "Nah. It'll be boring. Keep in touch."

She nodded and he closed the window as the car pulled away.

George, Rose and Callie watched it out of sight. As Callie turned to go back to the house Rose caught her sleeve.

“I want to show you something. It won’t take long.”

Callie followed her across the road and round the corner and Rose led her into the churchyard and stopped in front of a stone half-buried in the muddied turf.

“Here lies Agnes Soutar or Blair, born 13th August 1688, died October 12th 1756,” Callie read. “So she was ...”

“Sixty eight,” said Rose. “A good age for those days.”

“Do you think she really was a witch?”

“Witches don’t exist,” said Rose lightly. “But they used to say it passed through the female line, and you’re her daughter’s daughter’s daughter, etc.”

They looked at each other for a second before their gazes slid away.

“Come on, let’s go home.”

Thoughtfully, Callie followed her grandmother out of the churchyard.

We meant no harm.

Author's Note

Agnes Blair stepped out of my head and into this story, but Beatrix Laing, Janet Corphat and Patrick Morton were real people. Patrick denounced Beatrix, Janet and others to the real Minister Cowper for witchcraft in 1704. They were tried in Pittenweem in Fife in one of the last Scottish witch trials. Beatrix and Janet met with the fates described here. I don't know what happened to Patrick Morton.

You can find information about the Pittenweem Witch Trials – as I did – in *Fife History and Legend* by Raymond Lamont-Brown, and *Scottish Witches and Wizards* by Lily Seafield.

Constantine's Cave is real too. I read about it in *Fife History and Legend,* and am indebted to Alan Jeffreys of the Grampian Speleological Group and to Dr JLS Cobb for further information.

Thanks to my family for their patience with me, to Gale and Katy at Floris, and to Kathryn and Lindsey for their support.

Read on for an exciting extract of **Dark Spell**,
where Josh and Callie once again find themselves
fighting evil while Callie struggles to control
her newly discovered powers."

1. VALENTINE'S DAY

"Imagine what it must have been like," said Mr Davidson. "Kept in a dungeon for weeks, then dragged out and tied to a stake..." he paused for dramatic effect, "...and burned alive! That's what happened to George Wishart, just a few hundred metres away, in 1546. But why?"

He looked at the rows of faces in front of him, waiting in vain for some sort of response.

A hand went up.

"Yes, Evie?"

"Has anyone sent you a valentine card, sir?"

Mr Davidson flushed slightly. "This is a history lesson, Evie."

Evie Carroll gave a theatrical sigh. "I was only asking."

"You all live in St Andrews. Surely you know *something* about the history of the town?" Mr Davidson ploughed on determinedly.

The faces looking at him were perfectly blank. He swallowed nervously. There was a snigger from the back of the classroom.

Callie Hall, sitting near the back herself, thought, *Why are they doing this? He's only a student teacher, he hasn't done anything to them.*

"Come on, some of you must have ideas." Mr Davidson licked his lips and swallowed again.

It was like watching people torture a kitten. Callie felt her fingers start to tingle as her annoyance grew. She had had enough. She put down her pen which, strangely, kept rotating gently on the desk in front of her, and put up her hand to answer.

"It was religion," she said. "Protestants and Catholics."

Mr Davidson gave her a look of such naked gratitude that she was embarrassed. She looked down, caught sight of her pen, still turning by itself, and grabbed it.

"That's it exactly, Callie. Cardinal Beaton, who was Catholic, had Wishart, who was Protestant, burned as a heretic. But Wishart's friends took revenge..." He turned to write something on the board and half the class swivelled round to glare at Callie.

"You moron," hissed Jessica Langston. "Why did you spoil it?"

"She fancies him or something," said Evie under her breath. "*She* probably sent him a valentine card. She's such a loser."

Callie did her best to ignore them, and to ignore the prickling in her fingers, and stared at the board until the bell sounded for the end of the lesson and the start of lunchtime.

She contemplated eating outside somewhere, but although it was bright, it was pretty cold. It was only February after all.

The school cafeteria was full of girls giggling over valentine cards and eyeing up boys. Some of the boys were sniggering over cards too. Callie wondered fleetingly if Josh, her friend in Edinburgh, had sent anyone a card or got one himself. She couldn't imagine him behaving like these prats, but maybe he was different in Edinburgh to how he was here.

She found a quiet table and fished her lunch and a book out of her bag. She was absorbed in both when she heard a voice in front of her.

"Got a date with Davidson yet then?"

It was Evie, lunch tray in hand, backed by the rest of the posse that seemed to travel everywhere in her wake. They all wore matching sneers.

Evie put her tray down.

"Next time there's a plan, don't screw it up, you freak." She picked up her cup of water and threw it in Callie's face. "Oops. Sorry."

A ripple of laughter ran round the room as Evie picked up her tray.

Callie watched through her dripping hair as Evie walked away, anger building inside, fingers, hands, every inch of her tingling now.

At that moment Evie seemed to slip, though there was nothing on the floor: no pool of water, no smear of ketchup, no uneven floorboard. She screamed as she went down hard on her back, the contents of her tray flying up, then falling, to land with improbable accuracy all over her.

The posse squealed in horror and hurried to help her.

Callie dried her face and her long, brown braid of hair with her scarf, and went back to her lunch, ignoring the pool of water on the table in front of her.

"What did you do to her, freak?" Callie hadn't seen Jessica stomping over. "How did you make her fall?"

Callie felt heat rising in her face as she looked at

Jessica and beyond her to Evie, who was screeching and carrying on as the posse helped her to her feet. She seemed to be holding her wrist.

"How could I have made her fall? I was over here, you know that. She just slipped." Even as she said it, she could feel the treacherous prickling in her fingers again. *Not now, oh please, not now...*

The posse ushered the sobbing Evie past her, some of them shooting venomous glances at Callie.

"This is your fault, loser!" one of them shouted.

"I don't know what you did, freak, but we'll get you back for this. Just wait," Jessica spat at her as she turned to go.

Callie watched them leave, fighting the prickling, trying to calm herself. On the table, the spilled water bubbled and steamed unnoticed.